MURDER
ON BROADWAY

MURDER ON BROADWAY

EDWARD I. KOCH

and Wendy Corsi Staub

Concept created by Herbert Resnicow

KENSINGTON BOOKS

KENSINGTON BOOKS are published by

Kensington Publishing Corp.
850 Third Avenue
New York, NY 10022

Library of Congress Card Catalog Number: 96-076013
ISBN 1-57566-049-0

First Printing: July, 1996
10   9   8   7   6   5   4   3   2   1

Printed in the United States of America

MURDER
ON BROADWAY

ONE

As mayor of New York, I get invited to just about every noteworthy event within a twenty-mile radius of the Empire State Building. Some, I pass on. Others, I jump at.

For example, I always accept an invitation to a party when I know it's being catered by my pal Hinda Grisin of Fab Affairs, who does incredible things with wild mushrooms and goat cheese.

And I always accept when entertainment is involved. What could be better than sitting back and letting a bunch of talented performers transport you to another time and place, where you can forget the stress of running the world's most exciting city? It's total pleasure and relaxation—unless, of course, in the midst of the creative reverie, there's a murder . . .

No one does Broadway like Broadway.

Believe me, I know. Having traveled all over the world, and having seen various road productions of well-known plays and musicals, I'm confident that the cream of the theatrical crop is right here in New York City. Others come close, particularly a glitzy Andrew Lloyd Webber opening I once attended in London, but nothing can top seeing a big-time, razzle-dazzle show in one of the grand old theaters that dot the neighborhood we locals call Clinton. It's something I've always felt, and I never hesitate to say it. In fact . . .

"No one," I told my good friend Sybil Baker, as we stepped out of the limo on West Forty-sixth Street, "does Broadway like Broadway."

"So I've heard," she replied dryly, "every time I've accompanied you to one of these things."

I shrugged and offered her my arm. She took it and I glanced at the Regal Theater's brightly lit marquee above our heads. Its bold letters heralded tonight's tenth anniversary performance of the famed Nolan MacDougall musical, *The Last Laugh.*

Trailed, as usual, by the five NYPD sergeants who make up my bodyguard detail, we stepped onto the red carpet lain across the sidewalk for tonight's gala. I started to ask Sybil if she had a stick of gum, then blinked as a flashbulb exploded two inches from my face.

"For heaven's sake, Dayton," Sybil said to the youngish, shaggy-haired photographer, ducking the tripod slung over his shoulder. "Watch what you're doing with that thing. Someone could lose an eye."

As a veteran gossip columnist for Manhattan's number-one tabloid, the *Daily Register,* she obviously felt entitled to snap at the paper's underlings.

"Sorry, Sybil," the photographer said sheepishly, carefully tucking the tripod under his arm. "But listen—would you and the mayor mind staying put for a quick shot?"

She looked at me, and I shrugged. Better to pose and risk coming off stiff and unnatural than to have him catch me trying to loosen the shred of moo shu pork that had been lodged between my back teeth ever since our early dinner at the *Peking Duck* restaurant down in Chinatown.

Sybil and I obliged, standing with our arms around each other and smiling cheesily at the camera.

"How's my hair?" she asked, through clenched teeth.

I glanced at her and saw that every strand of her trademark orange bouffant was in place. "Perfect," I told her. "You look gorgeous, as usual."

Though she's famous for her writing, and her photo doesn't accompany her daily column, I seriously doubt that there's anyone in New York who wouldn't recognize Sybil. Not only is she still stunning at fiftysomething—with fine-boned features, snappy blue-green eyes, and the well-preserved figure of the Rockette she once was—but she's a fixture at charity balls, movie openings, fashion shows. You name it; if it's a celebrity-drawing event, she's there, shrewdly watching for a juicy tidbit of gossip to share with the world.

As the Dayton fellow took his picture of us, I saw that a few of the bystanders lining the velvet ropes were taking advantage and snapping their own shots.

"Who're they?" asked a woman clad in an *I Left My Heart in Des Moines* T-shirt.

"Must be some movie stars or something," I heard her Stetson-wearing male companion say. "Take their picture, Gertie. We can show the kids."

Sybil and I, accompanied by my Gang of Five, headed toward the row of glass doors that led into the Regal, one of the oldest and most ornate theaters in the district.

"Hey, Ed," someone shouted from the crowd. "Lookin' pretty snazzy."

"Thanks," I said, waving. I had on the new tux I'd gotten at Moe Ginsberg just last week. I grinned and asked, "How'm I doin'?"

"Great!" shouted a chorus of enthusiastic supporters.

"Lousy! What's up with the zoning delay for the new low-income housing complex in Astoria?" hollered a disgruntled voice.

There's one in every crowd.

"You'll find out," I informed him succinctly, "on tonight's eleven o'clock news. It'll be the top story. Obviously you missed my live press conference on the subject this afternoon."

With that, Sybil and I sailed into the air-conditioned lobby. Though it was early September, it had been incredibly hot and muggy outside, one of those stifling New York nights when you want to be down at *South Street Seaport,* catching a breeze off the East River and sitting in an open-air restaurant.

The blast of chilly air inside the lobby was pure heaven.

"Brrr," commented Sybil, promptly shivering.

I raised an eyebrow at her.

"Thin blood," she explained. "I'm always freezing."

"That dress doesn't help," I observed, eyeing her bare-shouldered, black Versace sheath that was cut short enough to reveal an expanse of her dancer's legs in dangerously high heels. It wasn't hard to imagine her in a Radio City kickline.

"If I'm cold during the show, I'll borrow your tux jacket," she decided.

"And start scandalous rumors?" I thought of poor Claude, Sybil's husband, whose job with the U.N. kept him globe-trotting much of the time. He never minded when I escorted his wife to some shindig, but he might not be thrilled if Sybil and I suddenly became a tabloid item.

"Listen, Ed," she said, *"I'm* the one who starts the scandalous rumors in this town."

"And you do it so well," I agreed, rocking back on my heels and looking around. The bodyguards were doing the same, their eyes shifting with expert scrutiny over the well-heeled crowd.

I immediately spotted twenty or more of my closest friends milling about, wearing the usual black tie and sequined getups suitable for a gala even such as this.

The faded, slightly shabby backdrop was a striking contrast to the glittering society crowd. Worn rose-colored silk panels covered the walls, framed by gilt moldings and antique filigree sconces that must once have held gaslights. In the corner by the ticket booth, there was a glass case filled with memorabilia—old programs, props, costumes, and yellowed reviews.

In honor of tonight's performance, the focal point in the lobby was a life-size picture of world-renowned composer Nolan MacDougall. It wasn't the best likeness of him—his teeth appeared rather protruding and his eyes were more squinty than usual.

I happened to know that MacDougall was one of the most vain-glorious men in an industry that's notorious for vanity, and I wondered how he'd reacted when he'd first glimpsed the unflattering photograph. Too bad I hadn't been there.

Nolan MacDougall, as you may have guessed, is hardly my favorite person. In fact, I can't think of many people I dislike more intensely. And I'm hardly alone in my loathing.

"What a pompous ass," Sybil muttered under her breath, nudging me with her elbow and gesturing at the flesh-and-blood incarnation of the composer, who stood a few feet from the photograph, regaling a cluster of bored-looking listeners with his ideas for a new musical.

"It's based on a classic fairy tale, of course," he was saying. "So many of today's most successful productions are."

"Shall we make our way over?" I asked, heaving a reluctant sigh.

"Might as well," Sybil replied. "I have to pick up some fodder for my column, and he's the best place to start. Though I'm sure I'm going to get an earful about something like the wallpaper patterns he's chosen for his new house in Saddle River."

I grinned, suspecting she was right. The man was forever bragging about his many real estate holdings, which included a Park Avenue duplex, a chalet in Aspen, a cottage in Tuscany.

Still, I marveled at how confident MacDougall appeared tonight. After all, it was no secret that *The Last Laugh* had been losing money lately, thanks to bad personal publicity and a series of casting changes, and that he'd staged this gala hoping to drum up some renewed interest in the show.

We hadn't taken two steps toward the swaggering composer when we were intercepted by a silver-haired, red-sequined whirlwind.

"Sybil, darling!" exclaimed Adriana Leek, her cheeks ruddy with excitement—and a liberal dollop of rouge. "How was your rock climbing trip to Vancouver?"

Did I mention that Sybil is ridiculously fit for her age? Every chance they get, she and Claude are off skiing in Colorado, diving in the Caribbean, or something equally adventurous.

"Vancouver was exciting," she told Adriana, "until I pulled a muscle in my calf. It was a week before I could walk normally again."

"Well, you are getting up there in years, darling," Adriana reminded her smugly. "It might be time to slow down a bit."

"Never!" Sybil harumphed.

"And Ed," Adriana turned to me, "it's wonderful to see you again. How was your vacation? I heard you were stricken with food poisoning after eating bad jambalaya."

When you're mayor of New York City, you can't get away with anything. "New Orleans was terrific, aside from that," I assured her. "Very relaxing."

"That's why they call it the Big Easy, I'm sure," Adriana declared, and glanced around, her dangling ruby earrings bouncing wildly. "Does anyone see Dimitri? I lost him someplace."

He was probably hiding. Lord only knew how a refined businessman like Dimitri Leek put up with a flibberty gibbet like Adriana. The woman never shut her mouth.

Which is why she's one of Sybil's favorite people.

While the two of them put their heads together, jabbering about some unsuspecting adulterer, I caught sight of Sebastian Nicolay and his wife. He and I spent some time in Congress together back in the early seventies; he representing a district in New Jersey, and I, of course, one in New York. He'd been defeated a few elections ago and was back in his law practice. I ran into him every now and then and always enjoyed his company. Like me, he was the kind of guy who isn't afraid to tell it like it is.

He caught my eye and waved me over.

"Ed, how have you been?" Sebastian asked. A bearded, brawny bear of a man, he looked distinctly uncomfortable in his tuxedo. "You remember Tetty."

"Of course." I shook their hands and told his wife she looked lovely, as usual, in her shimmering seashell-pink cocktail dress.

"Thank you," she said, and confided, "Tonight's an extraspecial occasion for me."

"That's because it's our twenty-fifth wedding anniversary," her husband said jovially.

I congratulated them, and Tetty Nicolay said, "Thank you, Mr. Mayor, but that wasn't what I meant. I'm especially thrilled to be here tonight because Conor Matthews is my godson."

"Conor Matthews?" I echoed blankly.

Then I recognized the name.

She was referring to the star of tonight's production, an actor who late last year had taken over the role from its longtime lead, Beau Walton. As I recalled, Walton had quit, amid much hoopla, to pursue a movie career. Apparently, he had yet to make a splash, since I'm a regular at the Orpheum multiplex a few blocks from

Gracie Mansion on East Eighty-eighth Street, and I hadn't seen him yet on the big screen.

"Conor's mother, Mindy, was my best friend when we were growing up in Montclair," confided Tetty Nicolay. "We met in Girl Scouts. She died, poor thing, when he was about seventeen. They were living in our guest house at the time, though Sebby and I were in the South of France celebrating our tenth wedding anniversary when it happened—oh, my, can you believe it's already been fifteen years now? Anyway, I've always felt terrible that we weren't there for the boy when—"

"Tetty!" Sebastian cleared his throat as if to warn her that she was rattling on, and I remembered that she has a tendency to do just that.

"Anyway," she said brightly, "Conor and I haven't really seen much of each other after all these years. He's made quite a name for himself in classical theater roles—he loves Shakespeare. But I'm a fan of big Broadway productions, myself, and I was thrilled when I read that he'd landed this part last fall."

"He's excellent in the role of Quincy Tate," I told her sincerely.

"You've seen him do it?"

"More than once. Actually, I've probably seen *The Last Laugh* a dozen times since it opened," I estimated, and watched her eyebrows shoot up.

"Why would you see the same show so many times?" Sebastian was looking at me like I was crazy.

"Whenever I entertain dignitaries from out of town, that's the thing they want to see," I said with a shrug. "That, or *Cats.*"

"Oh, *Cats.*" Sebastian rolled his eyes, and his wife slapped him playfully on the arm.

"What do you want? I'm allergic to cats," he said, and chuckled at his own wit.

"He's allergic to culture," Tetty told me. "But he does a good job of acting like he's interested, when he'd really rather be at a ball game."

"Well, I guarantee that you'll enjoy this show," I informed them, as the lobby lights dimmed briefly.

"Guess it's time to be seated," Tetty observed, and clutched her husband's arm.

I tracked down Sybil. She and Adriana Leek were having an animated conversation with a handsome young man who looked vaguely familiar.

He was lanky and had the kind of chiseled face that was suspiciously perfect, betraying a broad hint that he was no stranger to plastic surgery. His aquiline nose was a little too straight; the cleft in his chin a little too flagrant. And I had seen eyes that blue only once before—on my old housekeeper, Mamie Weiss, who had often lauded the discovery of colored contact lenses.

"Ed, there you are. This is Beau Walton," Sybil said, as Adriana drifted off to find Dimitri.

Belatedly, I recognized the face that I had, until now, seen only from below and beyond the footlights.

"We've met," he announced promptly, shaking my hand.

"We have?"

Walton looked insulted. "Of course. When you came backstage after one of my performances when I was playing Quincy."

"That's right," I agreed, though I had no recollection.

"You told me I was the most sublime actor who had ever graced the Broadway stage."

I seriously doubted that, but I nodded and murmured something appropriately flattering.

"And what are you doing now?" I couldn't resist asking.

"Actually, I'm between films, trying to decide which offer I should accept next," he said with the grace of one who wholeheartedly believes in his own excellence. "Though, of course, being a close friend of Nolan's, I wouldn't miss being here tonight, even if I were filming halfway around the world. It's hard to believe it's been ten years already since I immortalized the role of Quincy Tate."

On that note, Sybil cleared her throat. "I think it's time to go in."

"I'd better find Nolan," Beau said, and exited with a gallant wave.

"What a loser," Sybil said in my ear as we walked toward the theater. "He's bombing in the movie business. He'll be lucky if he finds work as an extra. Word has it, he's been talking to Mac-Dougall about returning to the cast of *The Last Laugh.*"

"Whose word?"

"Adriana's. And believe me, she would know. Her sister-in-law is sleeping with the assistant director's ex-husband."

I sighed. "Sybil . . ."

"Come on, Ed, this is my job."

She had a point.

My bodyguards took up posts around the theater, and I pitied their having to stand for the next four hours. Meanwhile, we were led to our seats by a smiling usher, who greeted us with a "Good evening, Mr. Mayor, Ms. Baker." He stopped at the entrance of the second row, center, handed over two programs, and cheerfully instructed us to enjoy the show.

"We certainly will from this spot," Sybil said, as we made our way down the row. She settled into her seat and said, "You rate, Ed. Whenever Claude and I attend one of these things, we're lucky if we're not in the last row."

"You're exaggerating," I told her. "You rate pretty high your-self, Ms. Baker."

"I do, but I'm not the mayor. These are the best seats in the house. Look, there's you-know-who," she said, bobbing her head toward the front row.

You-know-who turned out to be Harry Martin Tigue, the hottest actor to hit Hollywood in a decade. I had met him this past winter at a movie opening. The moment we were introduced, he'd declared himself a staunch conservative, and had looked at me as though I'd scurried out of a drain.

His hair, I noted snidely from my vantage point a row behind him, was thinning in back. And didn't he realize goatees were old news? Even I knew that.

"Look who he's with!" Sybil exclaimed, as the blonde at his side turned her head slightly to whisper in his ear.

"Who?"

"Courtney Phillips! Now *there*'s a scoop."

"Who?" I repeated absently, opening my program and deciding I'd had enough celebrity gossip for one night.

"You know, Courtney Phillips. She starred with him in his last movie. Her sister is *Lindsey* Phillips," Sybil added significantly.

Dawn broke, and I widened my eyes. "The Lindsey Phillips who recently—and successfully, I might add—sued Nolan MacDougall for breach of contract?"

"One and the same," Sybil verified, her eyes bright with the promise of relating this interesting development to the world in tomorrow's paper. "I can't believe this woman has the nerve to show up here, and sit in the front row bold as you please, after what her sister did to MacDougall."

"Since she won the case, I would think the issue is what *MacDougall* did to *her.*"

And what he had done, I recalled, was promise her the lead in his newest musical, *City Lights,* and then turn around and hire someone else, a Broadway veteran whose name escaped me now.

If I liked Nolan MacDougall, I might feel sorry for him, what with the lawsuit and the rapidly declining value of *The Last Laugh.* But since he was despicable, I had no sympathy.

"Look how both of them keep turning toward the camera," Sybil observed. "A couple of hams, aren't they?"

"What camera?" That shows how much of a ham *I* am, despite what some of my detractors say.

She pointed over our shoulders. "Tonight's performance is being taped for the Home Entertainment Network. They're going to show it on cable around the holidays."

For a minute or so, I watched Harry and Courtney pretending they had no idea they were being filmed, then tired of that and turned my attention to my *Playbill,* flipping to "Who's Who in the Cast."

I always like to scan the actors' biographies. As a theater buff, I usually realize that I've seen them in something somewhere before. Besides, *The Last Laugh* had several new cast members since I'd last seen the show. I read their biographies first, then turned to Conor Matthews's, reading it with renewed interest now that I knew he was Tetty Nicolay's godson.

According to his bio, he had been born in New Jersey and educated at the Royal Shakespeare Company in London. His credits included sundry summer stock and off-Broadway performances—all of them Shakespearean plays, I noticed. Tetty had said he was a dedicated fan of the Bard. His Broadway debut had been the lead in a revival of *Romeo and Juliet* that had opened and closed so quickly last year that I'd nearly forgotten about it.

Conor Matthews dedicated his Quincy Tate performance "to Kellie."

I suspected who she was a moment later, when I read the biography of the beautiful blond actress playing the female lead, a character named Amber Blue. According to the blurb in *Playbill*, Kellie Farrell had gotten her start in commercials, and most notably, had originated the role of "Heather Kingston" on the daytime soap *The Midnight Hour*. She must be the Kellie that Conor Matthews had mentioned. I idly speculated that they might be real-life lovers.

Sybil would know, but before I could turn to ask her, the lights went down, the curtain went up, and a hush fell over the audience.

Settling back in my seat, I prepared to lose myself in the pre-Depression vaudeville era.

The Last Laugh revolved around the lives and loves of a troupe of performers. Quincy Tate was the focal point, a man whose wiseacre comedy routine hid a tragic life. He was desperately infatuated with Amber Blue, never suspecting that the ingenue was only using him to become a star.

Having seen the show so many times, and owning a CD of the soundtrack, I knew the musical numbers—not to mention most of the dialogue—by heart. Naturally, I fully expected to enjoy the performance.

Maybe it was the heartburn that was stealing over me from too many fried wontons dipped in hot Chinese mustard.

Or maybe it was that something was off in the rhythm of the show itself.

In any case, I just couldn't seem to get caught up in what was happening onstage. Even the big production number midway through the first act, where a vintage Packard is driven onstage during an all-out song-and-dance routine, didn't capture my full attention.

Instead, although I mentally sang along with the familiar tunes from the show, I found my mind wandering to the speech I had to write for tomorrow morning's breakfast with a Harlem church choir that had been winning national acclaim. I wondered if they'd be serving bagels, cream cheese, and lox. Hopefully not.

Don't get me wrong. I grew up on the stuff; I love it as much as the next New Yorker. But according to Hiram Schnegel, M.D., if I don't lay off the rich stuff, I might not be around to lead New York into the new millennium, something I've publicly sworn I'll do.

Moo shu pork and fried wontons won't get me there—to say nothing of the tongue on seedless rye I'd had for lunch this afternoon. I'd done the honors at a ribbon-cutting ceremony for a new Kosher deli in Midwood down in Brooklyn. And how could I refuse the sandwich they'd named after me?

I vowed, as the curtain came down on Act One, to have one of my aides arrange for the Harlem choir people to serve me half a grapefruit, which is my usual breakfast these days—when I'm behaving.

"What did you think?" Sybil asked, turning to me as the lights came up and the audience stirred.

"So-so," I said truthfully.

"Exactly. It's Conor Matthews. He seems distracted. I wonder if having Beau Walton in the audience is making him nervous," she mused, glancing over to where Walton, MacDougall, and other VIPs were slipping out of their front row seats.

I followed Sybil into the aisle and out toward the lobby. It goes without saying that you don't stay in your seat during intermission when you're attending a gala performance with Manhattan's premier gossip columnist.

"Sybil, are you enjoying the show?" trilled a voice at my elbow as Sybil and I waited in line at the bar.

I turned and saw Rebecca Blodgette-Miller, a British-born aristocrat who had married into one of America's most prominent acting families.

Word had it that her own folks back in London had all but disowned her for hobnobbing with the show biz crowd. Not that she seemed to mind. Rebecca was the kind of woman who always appeared to be having a fabulous time, and tonight was no exception. She was draped in black satin and her head was wrapped in some sort of sparkly, feathery headdress. Rebecca was nothing if not dramatic.

Apparently, she didn't see me standing there or realize that Sybil and I were together.

Her kohl-rimmed eyes were big and round as she leaned toward Sybil and whispered, "Have you ever seen anything like it?"

"Like what?"

"Conor Matthews, of course. The poor man is a bloody basket case. He and the divine Ms. Farrell are reportedly on the outs—as if we couldn't tell. You'd think they could conjure some chemistry for our sake!"

So I'd been right about the leading man and his leading lady. Well, when it comes to noticing details and making deductions, I'm as sharp as they come.

Sybil's ears had perked up at that tasty morsel, and she coyly asked, "Trouble in paradise? I had no idea. Last I heard, they were engaged."

Apparently, I was the only one who hadn't been aware, before this evening, that Matthews and Farrell were an item. I continued to eavesdrop, though I'm sure I appeared intently focused on obtaining a glass of wine before the lights dimmed again.

"That's history, dear Sybil," Rebecca was saying. "Now, this is all very hush-hush, but according to Adam"—that would be her well-connected movie star husband—"life is imitating art."

"You mean she's using him to enhance her career," Sybil clarified, as familiar with the plot of *The Last Laugh* as I am.

"That's not all."

"She's dating one of their costars behind his back?"

"You didn't hear it from me. Adam would ring up his divorce lawyer in a flash if he knew I'd spilled the beans."

"Of course I didn't hear it from you," Sybil concurred. "Who is it?"

"I gave you a clue when I said life imitates art. And that, love, is all I have to say on the subject. Have you heard that I'm jetting off to Morocco tomorrow?"

Sybil murmured that no, she hadn't heard.

"I'm visiting hubby on location. Should be blissful. Well, ta-ta."

With that, Rebecca sailed off through the glass doors to have a cigarette with the crowd of smokers on the sidewalk.

Sybil turned to me. "Quick, Ed, let me see your program."

"Where's yours?"

"I left it on my seat."

I handed my *Playbill* over with a sigh, knowing exactly what she was up to, but not letting on.

Sure enough, she flipped to the cast list, checking to see who was playing Hugo Shields.

The character, of course, is Quincy Tate's chief showbiz rival. He wins Amber's heart, since she naturally doesn't see that he's a pompous, calculating jerk.

Not only that, but he's ruthless. In one of the final scenes of the show, the one where Hugo is supposed to shoot Quincy as part of their routine, he replaces the blanks with real bullets. Of course, as Quincy lays dying in Amber's arms, she realizes that she's loved him all along.

Needless to say, Nolan MacDougall isn't known for writing happy endings.

"A *ha!*" Sybil pointed a perfectly manicured index finger at the program. "Wesley Fisk."

"Pardon?"

"Wesley Fisk," she informed me, "is the actor playing Hugo Shields. He and Kellie Farrell are fooling around."

"You don't know that for sure, Sybil."

"I'm ninety-nine percent sure, and by the time the evening is out, I'll have verified that information, Ed."

I had no doubt that she would.

We spent the remainder of the intermission sipping a delightful Merlot and mingling on the mezzanine.

I managed to set up a meeting with a NoHo developer who's been eluding my phone calls for the past month. That coup, to say nothing of the wine, left me with a warm glow as Sybil and I returned to our seats for Act Two.

This time, armed with my knowledge of the behind-the-scenes love triangle, I managed to focus more intently on the production. I knew the show well enough to notice that Conor Matthews dropped several lines, and delivered the rest in a distracted manner.

For her part, Kellie Farrell was a pro, as was Wesley Fisk. They were certainly convincing in the scene where their characters declare their love for each other in passionate whispers as the unsuspecting Quincy slumbers nearby.

Conor Matthews, however, wasn't even convincing as someone who was asleep. I could see his face twitching and his leg jittering beneath the blanket that covered him.

I caught sight of Dolph Schwartz, the *Register*'s theater critic, sitting in the front row and scribbling furiously in a notebook. That didn't bode well for tomorrow's review, and I found myself pitying poor Matthews.

At last, the final scene began.

I stifled a yawn behind my hand, then checked my watch. I estimated that I'd be back at Gracie Mansion, climbing into bed, inside the hour.

The tragedy unfolding onstage sizzled with tension, and for the first time all evening, Conor Matthews seemed to have thrown his heart into his acting. I found myself drawn into his plight, into the play-within-a-play, as he portrayed a desperate man who was portraying a desperate man.

"Go ahead," he urged the dastardly Hugo Shields when he finally brandished a pistol. "Shoot me. I dare you."

I braced myself for the sound of fake gunshots. And even though I was prepared, I found myself wincing when the incredibly realistic staccato blasts erupted onstage.

I watched Matthews crumple to the ground, bleeding profusely from a wound in his chest. Kellie Farrell, rushing to gather him into her arms, was appropriately horrified. Wesley Fisk was satisfyingly smug, then dismayed as he realized Amber Blue had true feelings for the dying Tate.

I marveled at how real the fake blood looked, spattered over Matthews's baggy plaid suit and seeping across the wooden stage floor. Special effects never cease to amaze me.

I stretched, tucked my *Playbill* into my pocket, and prepared to applaud as soon as the last line had been uttered.

But instead of murmuring "You'll always be my only love," Kellie Farrell was shrieking, "Oh my God, he's really been shot!"

Had she lost it? I wondered. That was an exact replay of the line she'd uttered only moments before . . .

But this time, she wasn't following it up with "Quincy, Quincy, no!" Instead, she was screaming, "Conor, Conor, no . . ."

When the house lights came up abruptly and a furor erupted onstage, I realized, along with the rest of the audience, what had happened.

Life had, indeed, imitated art.

_____ TWO

The scene was sheer bedlam—half the audience storming toward the stage, the better to witness the gruesome drama that was unfolding; the rest fleeing toward the exits, as though fearing that they would be the gunman's next targets.

Never mind that the gunman, a stunned-looking Wesley Fisk, had been grabbed by two of my bodyguards, who were leading him off the stage.

The other three guards had materialized at my side, surrounding me—and a protesting Sybil—protectively.

"I have to get up there," she told Mohammed Johnson, who had effectively blocked her with his bulky six-foot-six frame. He ignored her, speaking into the hand-held radio he'd plucked from his pocket.

And anyway, by now the curtain had come down and the Regal's security guards were ordering the audience away from the stage.

"We have to get you out of here, Mayor," said Lou Sabatino, his eyes darting around the room. The wail of sirens could be heard out in the street.

After a brief conversation, my guards prepared for action.

"There's an exit backstage that leads to an alley," Mohammed said. "That would be the best option. I'm having the limo brought around the block. Let's go."

I nodded, anxious to see what was happening behind the scenes.

Sybil, of course, was practically chomping at the bit in her eagerness to get back there.

I'm always amazed at how effective my gang is when they move me through a crowd, magically gaining access to off-limits sites. We were swept past the theater security guards posted along the edge of the stage, up a short flight of stairs, and through a door.

We were ushered down a musty-smelling hallway, past flights of steps leading both up and down, to another door. We walked through that and found ourselves in the cavernous, drafty wings.

I immediately spotted Kellie Farrell. The diminutive blonde was convulsed in tears, sitting on the floor. Her 1920s-style costume was covered in blood, and she was clutching a towel she'd evidently used to wipe it off her hands. Standing over her were two uniformed NYPD detectives.

The entire area was swarming with cops by now, and I saw that the theater security guards had sealed off the two exits. Until this moment, I had vaguely assumed that what had happened was some kind of freak accident.

Suddenly, though, I realized the implications. Just like in the plot of *The Last Laugh,* someone could have—must certainly have—replaced the blanks with real bullets.

Which meant the NYPD had a possible homicide on their hands.

Dazed-looking cast and chorus members stood in tight, anxious little clusters, their gaudy period costumes and stage makeup appearing garish in the bright overhead lights. A few of them were weeping; others looked terrified.

The crew, distinguished by their red "The Last Laugh: Tenth Anniversary Performance" T-shirts, milled about, and I saw a few of them being questioned by the police.

Meanwhile, paramedics kept scurrying by, and judging by the grim looks on all of their faces, I guessed the prognosis for Conor Matthews wasn't very good.

"Since the exits are sealed, we'd better stay put right here," I told Lou, stopping a few feet from the anguished Kellie Farrell.

"You're right. The police will want to question everyone before anyone's allowed to leave the building. Even though you're the mayor, you'll want to cooperate and be interviewed—of course as soon as we can get you out of here, we will."

I shrugged and saw that Sybil's eyes were gleaming as she looked about the wings. I recognized that shrewd expression.

I leaned over and whispered, "What kind of ghoul are you? A man's been shot, and here you are, sniffing around for gossip."

"I'm a ghoul whose job doesn't cease to exist when tragedy strikes," she retorted in a low voice. "Believe me, my heart goes out to that poor kid onstage. But that doesn't mean I'm going to ignore a golden opportunity like this."

I've always gotten along very well with the press, better than most politicians. But I have to admit, there are times when I'm fed up with blood-sniffing journalists—even when they are my closest and dearest friends.

"Sybil," I snapped, "you're sick."

She raised her hands as if to say she couldn't argue with that, then managed to slip away while my guards' heads were momentarily turned. Since their job was to guard me, but not necessarily my companions, they didn't appear overly concerned when they noticed that she was missing.

Meanwhile, I turned my attention to Kellie Farrell. Someone had handed her a mirror, and she was wiping her eyes, carefully dabbing at the muddy mascara, shadow, and liner that streaked her cheeks.

The woman had just seen her lover—or *ex*-lover—gunned down in cold blood. Now, though she continued weeping and carrying on, she appeared more than a little concerned with her appearance.

Hmm.

This wasn't the first time I'd been close to a possible homicide. In fact, I pride myself on having solved the murder of millionaire real estate mogul Karl Krieg not so long ago. After that, I'd vowed to leave detective work to New York's finest.

But I'll admit that in that moment when I glimpsed Kellie Farrell carefully wiping her makeup, I mentally labeled her Suspect Number One.

My mind raced back to what Rebecca Blodgette-Miller had implied during intermission, about how Kellie was two-timing Conor . . .

With Wesley Fisk.

Bingo. Suspect Number Two, I concluded, glancing about to

see him perched on a chair by the edge of the stage as two police detectives continued to question him. He was pale and appeared agitated. His eyes kept darting in Kellie's direction.

"Well, if it isn't Mayor Koch!" A familiar voice caught my attention, and I turned to see my old pal Charley Deacon striding toward me.

Before he was promoted to lieutenant, he was one of my bodyguards. In fact, he'd been guarding me the night of Karl Krieg's murder, which had taken place down at City Hall during a wedding ceremony I was performing.

"Charley, how's it going?"

"Man, I just had a flash of déjà vu," he said, halting in front of me and shaking my hand.

"Meaning . . . ?"

"You seem to have been a key player in a similar situation once before, Mayor."

"Are you implying that I had something to do with this, Charley?" I joked, knowing that was about as far-fetched as my committing the Krieg murder.

Although, there had been a time, I recalled, when I was considered a suspect . . .

Ridiculous, of course.

"Nah, you're clean," Charley assured me with a grin, and then his expression turned somber. I noticed that his chestnut-colored skin glistened with sweat, and he wiped a trickle from his hairline. He must have been onstage under the hot lights, watching them work on Matthews.

"The kid didn't make it," he told me. "We've got a homicide on our hands."

I shook my head sadly, pitying the Matthews's family. Such a shame. Then I remembered poor Tetty Nicolay, so proud and obviously fond of her godson.

"Charley," I said, "have you seen Sebastian Nicolay and his wife anywhere?"

"Who?"

"He used to be a Jersey congressman—remember? I introduced you to him last year at Sotheby's."

"Oh, I remember. No, I haven't seen him tonight. Why?"

"Because Conor Matthews was Tetty Nicolay's godson, and they were in the audience. The poor woman must be going out of her mind."

"I'll go find her. We'll need to question her," Charley said, and strode away.

I spotted Sybil sidling toward Nolan MacDougall and Beau Walton, who were conversing emphatically with several detectives who had their backs to me. I decided to join her—not, of course, because I was nosing around for gossip, but because despite my earlier intentions, I could very likely assist the police in solving this case.

After all, I had the edge—while they'd been scattered about the city going about their police business, I'd been in the audience, watching the performance leading up to the tragic murder.

When I reached the group—naturally, dogged by Lou, Paul, and Mohammed—Nolan caught sight of me. "Gentlemen," he announced, "here's the mayor. Perhaps he can be of service. I believe he was prominently seated in the audience, close enough to have noted anything out of the ordinary that may have happened onstage."

"I'm Detective David Rabinowitz, Mr. Mayor," the short, pudgy investigator said with what appeared to be a shadow of a smirk. "I believe we've met."

He did look familiar. "Probably," I agreed. "Jog my memory, will you?"

"A mutual acquaintance—Ken Brooks," he said, and instantly, it came back to me . . . along with a decidedly unpleasant taste in my mouth.

I'd had a run-in with Rabinowitz over Brooks, a fellow police detective and Rabinowitz's former partner. Brooks had been dismissed from the force last spring after several accusations of brutality.

I had actively and vocally supported the decision to remove his badge, to the anger of quite a few members of the NYPD who thought he was innocent. Rabinowitz was the most outspoken of them, showing up at a press conference to inform me that "a guy like Ken would never be capable of the vile acts you have unfairly linked to him." He then had the nerve to call me a bleeding heart.

I, in turn, advised him to wake up and smell the coffee—though not in those polite terms. I had heard from reliable sources in the department that some tourist had caught Brooks on camcorder, beating a twelve-year-old boy he'd caught picking someone's pocket at the St. Patrick's Day parade.

Sure enough, a month after my run-in with Rabinowitz, the videotape surfaced, proving beyond a doubt that Ken Brooks was a lowlife thug who had gotten what he deserved.

People would save themselves a lot of headaches if they'd listen when I try to tell them something. Unfortunately, not everyone listens when the mayor speaks.

When I'm wrong, I'm always willing to admit it. And when I'm right, I'm the first to say, "I told you so."

I would have said it to Rabinowitz, only this didn't seem like the proper time or place.

So all I said was, "Good to see you again, Detective."

He looked surprised—not to mention relieved. "And this," he said, "is Detective Joanne Swanson." He gestured at his tall, blond partner, whose hair was pinned in a tight coiled braid and whose attractive face was scrubbed bare of makeup. "We were just asking Mr. MacDougall and Mr. Walton whether they noticed anything unusual—"

"Aside from the fact that Matthews's performance was undeniably dreadful," Beau Walton smoothly inserted.

I mentally labeled him Suspect Number Three, then told the detectives, "Actually, Matthews *did* seem distracted. I've seen the show several times in the past, and I noticed that he dropped quite a few lines and missed some cues."

"We've established that," Swanson said with a nod. "We've already questioned the director, his assistant, and the stage manager, as well as a few members of the crew. All of them told us that Matthews, who is usually an unflappable pro, was unusually subdued and seemed nervous this evening. What we need to know is *why.*"

Sybil and I exchanged a glance. When she said nothing, I spoke up. "You might want to ask Kellie Farrell and Wesley Fisk, gentlemen."

"Kellie Farrell?" Swanson echoed, and glanced in her direction.

Her back was to us, but it appeared that she was still crying inconsolably, surrounded by a group of cast members who patted her shoulders in an effort to comfort her.

"She's Matthews's fiancée," Rabinowitz told his partner. "She's being closely questioned. Do you happen to know, Mayor, whether their relationship was troubled?"

"Of course it wasn't troubled," MacDougall interjected, as if that were the most preposterous notion he'd ever heard. "Their engagement was announced in the *Times* just this past week."

Again, I glanced at Sybil. Her mouth was set in a firm line, as though she was determined not to reveal what she knew, or her source. She'd given her word to Rebecca, and I happen to know that for all her faults, Sybil's word is always good. She never betrays a source.

I shrugged and told the detectives, "It seems logical that if Matthews was upset over something, his romance with Miss Farrell is a likely possibility. After all, I saw the performance, and their chemistry definitely left something to be desired."

"And Wesley Fisk?" Swanson asked, scribbling something in her notebook.

"Oh, come on! He may have *shot* Matthews," Nolan MacDougall piped up, mopping his face with a handkerchief, "but that was part of the show. It doesn't mean he had anything to do with the fact that—"

"I didn't say that he did," Swanson interrupted. "But we fully intend to thoroughly question everyone involved in this production, Mr. MacDougall, and we would appreciate your cooperation."

MacDougall threw his hands up and blurted, "By all means, Detective. Anything I can do to help, just let me know. I just can't believe this is happening to me. Do you realize what big news this is? It's going to be the headline in every paper in the world tomorrow morning."

Rabinowitz and Swanson exchanged a fleeting glance.

So did Sybil and I.

"Maybe not every paper in the *world*," MacDougall quickly amended. "But it *is* huge news."

"That, it is," Walton agreed, laying a hand on his shoulder. "Come on, Nolan, let's get you a seat and a glass of water."

MacDougall looked at the detectives, as if to ask their permission.

"Go ahead," Rabinowitz said. "But not far away. I have more questions for you. *Both* of you."

As soon as they'd left, Sybil asked briskly, "Is MacDougall a suspect, Detective?" She may as well have whipped out a notebook and taken a pencil from behind her ear.

Rabinowitz blinked. "Who, may I ask, are you?"

She looked insulted. "Sybil Baker," she said curtly. "I'm with the *Daily Register.*"

His nose wrinkled in slight but obvious disdain. "I see. And just how did you get backstage?"

"I'm Ed's date," Sybil told them, a tad haughtily. She linked her arm through mine.

They looked at me. I nodded reluctantly.

"Getting back to Wesley Fisk," Rabinowitz said after a beat, "why do you suggest that we speak with him about Matthews's being upset tonight?"

"I just thought that he and Kellie Farrell were especially convincing in the scene where she two-timed Quincy Tate—that would be Conor Matthews."

Both detectives looked thoughtful.

"Excuse me," Mohammed said, discreetly appearing at my side. "But the mayor has been cleared to leave. His car is waiting."

"I assume that means you'll be leaving, too, Ms. Baker," Rabinowitz said pointedly to Sybil.

"Yes, it does," I agreed, before she could protest. "If you would like to question me further, Detective, I can be reached at my office at City Hall—or you can have Charley Deacon track me down."

With that, Sybil and I were escorted by all five of my bodyguards to the door, where a uniformed security guard was standing sentinel. He stepped aside to let us pass, opening the door to the alley.

I hadn't anticipated that the press would already have staked out every entrance to the Regal. Instantly, we were greeted by a storm of shouted questions and popping flashbulbs, not to mention the glaring lights from video film crews representing every news program in the city.

"Mr. Mayor, what do you know about Conor Matthews's condition?" shouted one reporter.

"Is he dead?" another one hollered bluntly.

"I'm positive," I said, as the crowd quieted instantly to hear what I had to say, "that someone will be making an official statement to you at some point. I have no comment."

"How was the show? Did you enjoy it?" some idiot quipped, and I glared.

"Don't be an ass, Ralph," Sybil barked—apparently the question had come from a *Register* reporter.

She clung to my arm as my bodyguards shouldered a path through the alley toward the back of the theater. The night air was hot and close, and you could feel the heat radiating from the concrete surrounding us. We crossed a small, jammed, trash-strewn parking lot and walked through another shadowy alley between two buildings.

We emerged on the sidewalk out on Forty-seventh Street. I immediately spotted my official limo, with the usual unmarked black sedan behind it.

Three of my bodyguards jumped into the first sedan, and Paul and Lou got into the second one with Sybil and me.

As soon as we'd settled ourselves inside, Kevin Teirney, the NYPD officer who was doing the driving this evening, turned and asked, "Geez, what the heck happened in there, Mr. Mayor? I was parked near the theater on Forty-sixth, waiting for you, when all hell broke loose. Cops, rescue vehicles, you name it. At first I thought someone had taken a shot at you, what with that press conference you gave in Queens this afternoon and everything. Gave me a helluva scare."

I cringed, remembering the surly man who'd questioned me about the low-income housing deal as I was entering the theater earlier. Sometimes it was all too easy to realize how hostile some citizens are—and how vulnerable I really am.

But I've learned not to dwell on the downside of public office, so I assumed a casual expression and said, "Nah, I'm still here to drive you nuts, Teirney."

"Lucky me. So what did happen? Mohammed radioed me to

drive around the block—took me almost forty minutes. I haven't seen this neighborhood so mobbed since the Macy's parade."

"One of the actors was shot," I told him, glancing out the window as he headed toward Seventh Avenue. The sidewalk was crowded with the usual cab-seeking after-theater crowd.

"Oh yeah? He make it?"

"Nope."

"That's a shame." Teirney shook his head. His voice held the matter-of-fact detachment of a cop who'd seen too much, and accepted that the world can be pretty damn bleak. "Did they catch the perp?"

"Nope," I said again, my mind zinging back to what I'd witnessed backstage.

"You're kidding. How'd he get away with it?"

While Sybil and the others filled him in, I sat there and went over my mental list of suspects once again.

Kellie Farrell.

Wesley Fisk.

Beau Walton.

Which of them was the guilty party? Or was it someone else, someone who also had access to the gun . . . and a reason to want Conor Matthews dead?

Only one thing was certain, I concluded as we crossed Broadway and rounded the corner onto Seventh Avenue just above Times Square . . .

It was time, once again, for Ed Koch, Mayor Extraordinaire, to transform into Ed Koch, Detective Extraordinaire.

THREE

In all the commotion Saturday night, I had forgotten to arrange for the Harlem choir to serve me just grapefruit for breakfast.

Naturally, I couldn't pass up a still-warm everything-flavored bagel smeared with rich, scallion-dotted cream cheese and piled high with fresh, firm-fleshed orange-pink Nova Scotia lox.

Not when it was sitting right in front of me.

And not when the littlest choir member, a braided charmer named Jaleesa, tugged my sleeve and piped up, "I fixed it up for you all by myself, Mr. Mayor. Just the way you like it. Go ahead, have a big bite."

And so it was that I arrived back at Gracie Mansion feeling pleasantly full—and unpleasantly guilty. I vowed to myself—and to Hiram Schnegel, M.D.—that lunch would consist of seltzer and a salad. No dressing, no cheese, no croutons.

The first thing I did at home was head to my bedroom and change from my suit into a pair of lightweight khaki chinos and a short-sleeved cotton shirt.

Then I headed for my home office, where a thick stack of Sunday newspapers waited. I had almost two hours before I had to be downtown to drop in on a charity dance-athon that had been going on since Friday night. They wanted me to make a little speech and congratulate the noble winners, who by that time probably wouldn't care if the Pope stopped by to commend them. I could do a mean jitterbug when pressed, but forty-eight hours of dancing was my idea of torture.

I turned on all the lights in my office. It was a gray, muggy afternoon with thunderstorms predicted. Judging by how dark the sky was, it could start pouring any second.

I settled in my chair with my feet on the desk and started skimming through the papers.

Sure enough, the murder of Conor Matthews was front-page news, and not just locally. Every article I read made mention of the many celebrities and dignitaries who had attended the performance.

Of course, as mayor, I was pictured in several of the New York papers. Rather than use the upbeat photos that had been snapped as Sybil and I made our way into the theater via the red carpet, every editor had chosen to show us making our back-door escape.

So there I was, looking disturbed and irritated with the press as I was caught by a gazillion cameras. And there was Sybil, clinging to my arm in the *Register*'s photo, though she had, of course, been cropped out of the pictures in rival tabloids.

Hizzoner Flees Scene of Crime, trumpeted one photo tag line, much to my dismay.

Another read, *Is Koch A Curse?* That one was accompanied by a blurb that made mention of my presence at the City Hall wedding where Karl Krieg had been murdered.

The intercom on my desk rang just as I was grumbling and tossing the offending newspaper aside.

"Mr. Mayor? I have Sybil Baker on the line," said Carmen, a charming woman who had joined the Gracie Mansion staff just this week.

"Put her through," I said, after only a moment's hesitation.

Not that I was in the mood for her brand of chatter, but Sybil would know I was home, and she was the sort of person who would give poor Carmen a hard time if she refused to put her through. I like to think I'm a caring boss, and the least I could do was spare a rookie that kind of irritation.

Sybil greeted me with a blurted, "Did you see the paper?"

"Which one?"

"The *Register*, of course," she replied in a tone that asked, *Is there any other?*

"I glanced at it, yes. Haven't read it yet."

"Nice picture of us, isn't it?"

I sifted through the papers until I found the right photo again. That one was accompanied by a line that read, *Mayor Ed Koch escorts the* Daily Register's *own Sybil Baker to the gala—then flees from the gore.*

I grunted into the phone at Sybil, who went on, "Did you see my column?"

"Not yet. Why?"

"Read it," she ordered. "I'll wait."

With a sigh, I flipped to her usual page and started scanning the italic type. The murder, of course, was the main topic of her column.

I scanned the paragraphs, which mostly discussed the notable members of the audience, then said, "You didn't mention that Matthews and Kellie Farrell were on the outs."

"No, I didn't." She sounded smug.

"Why not?"

She hesitated, then told me, "It just didn't seem right. I didn't want to imply that Kellie Farrell—or even worse, Wesley Fisk—had anything to do with the murder."

"I thought it was your job to do just that."

Clearly miffed, she retorted, "It's my job to entertain my readers with gossip, not to finger suspects in a murder case."

I was just about to commend her on her admirable attitude when she added, "Besides, if I mention what I heard, I'll have the cops breathing down my neck, asking me how I know. And I can't reveal my source. Adam Miller just got back on his feet after that scandal with his son being involved in an L.A. drug bust. The last thing Adam needs is to be dragged into a murder investigation. And Rebecca's marriage to him is on shaky ground as it is. I don't want to be responsible for his divorcing her. Besides, the last thing *I* need is for Rebecca to lose access to the gossip Adam feeds her—and for me to lose access to Rebecca. She's a staple of my column. You wouldn't believe the dirt I get from her."

I rolled my eyes, nodded, and started to ask her what her point was.

"Anyway," she went on, cutting me off, "I know you, Ed. You're planning to do some digging, to see what you can find out. Use the inside info about Farrell and Fisk to get an edge on the cops, and you'll have the case solved before they've finished filling out the initial paperwork. I didn't like those two detectives, Rabinowitz and Swanson."

I didn't tell her that I was sure the feeling was mutual. Nor did I mention that Rabinowitz and I weren't exactly old pals.

Instead, I said, "For one thing, Sybil, I'm sure that the detectives are already considering Farrell and Fisk. And for another, I don't think it's that simple. It's obvious to me that both of them had motives, but so did a few other people I can think of."

"Beau Walton," she said promptly.

"Why do you say that?"

"Everyone knows his movie career is washed up. He'd be a fool not to realize his mistake and want to come back to *The Last Laugh*. And he didn't strike me as the nicest guy I've ever met. Bump off his replacement so that he could step back into the role of Quincy Tate? I wouldn't put it past him."

I wouldn't either, but I didn't tell her that.

"And then," she continued, "there's the esteemed Nolan Mac-Dougall."

"MacDougall?" I echoed, leaning back in my leather chair thoughtfully. "What makes you say that?"

"Oh, Ed, please. Did you notice the way he was going on about the press this was going to get?"

"Actually, I did. *Bad* press," I clarified.

At the time, I'd been shocked that even a narcissist like Mac-Dougall could be so blatantly self-absorbed in the midst of a tragedy.

"As far as MacDougall's concerned," Sybil informed me, "any press about this show is *good* press at this stage of the game. Think about it, Ed. Every newspaper in the country—and a lot of entertainment magazines and trades, too—are going to jump all over this story. That means a barrage of free publicity for *The Last Laugh*.

Publicity Nolan MacDougall couldn't *buy*—even if he had the money. Which he doesn't, thanks to Lindsey Phillips."

Lindsey Phillips. The actress who had sued MacDougall.

I had to hand it to Sybil. It made sense.

So much sense that I found myself asking her, "What are you doing tomorrow night?"

"Watching the Giants on Monday Night Football," she answered promptly.

I recalled that Sybil is a die-hard sports fan, and that the new football season was underway.

"At the Meadowlands?" I asked her.

"Nope, on TV. They're out of town. So I'm free until the game starts at nine," she added. "Why?"

"Never mind." I had thought better of my whim, but it was too late.

"Tell me, Ed," Sybil commanded.

"I was just thinking . . ." I began reluctantly, "that maybe . . . I don't know . . ."

"We could get together and play Nick and Nora?"

Either Sybil had read my mind, or she's even sharper than I'd given her credit for. In either case, it couldn't hurt to brainstorm with her.

On one condition.

"I *did* have something like that in mind," I admitted, "but only if you agree not to slip *anything* into your column about the case— and me."

"Nothing?"

"Nothing. The last thing I want is for the entire city to find out I'm working on another homicide."

"Why? The Krieg case gave you a boost in the polls."

"I *solved* that one, Sybil. If I start investigating the Matthews case, and I don't come up with anything, what do you think that'll do to me in the polls?"

"I see what you're saying."

"Not to mention that the NYPD has taken a few slams in the press lately. I don't think they'd appreciate any publicity about the mayor doing their work for them. And another thing," I said, "is that I don't want to make any of the suspects suspicious of *me*. I'd rather have them off guard when I approach them, so they won't realize what I'm really up to. Got it?"

"Got it," she said grudgingly. "But when this is over, and you've nabbed the killer—"

"*If* I've nabbed the killer," I cut in.

"Not if, *when*," she responded. "You know damn well you're going to crack the case, Ed. You have a flair for investigative work."

"You're right," I agreed, flattered that she'd noticed. "Okay, what happens *when* I solve the case?"

"I get an exclusive for the *Register.*"

I groaned. "Sybil . . ."

"Come on, Ed. I have access to sources you'd never uncover on your own. People in the theater industry. People who probably know something . . ."

She had me, as usual.

"Okay, it's a deal," I finally told her.

After all, a little positive press never hurt anyone—particularly a mayor.

Seven-thirty Monday morning found me at my City Hall office in lower Manhattan, ready to work my way through a series of meetings with various city officials, as well as through my usual cup after cup of coffee.

With me, coffee is a singular experience. It has to be very hot, very strong. It has to be black. And, above all, it has to be my brand—Martinson's. The wonderful woman who had been my secretary for all these years, Rosemary Larkin, had known that about me.

When she retired in June, I had to get used to her replacement, Maria Perez. Maria, unlike Rosemary, has no interest in making coffee; which is fine with me, since I make the best coffee this side of the East River—not that I'd go around telling Rosemary Larkin, who might beg to differ.

In any event, I am now—by my own choice—solely responsible, every morning, for making my own coffee in the kitchenette ádjoining my office. And that was the first thing I did today, upon arriving at work.

The second thing I did was settle in at my prized desk, which had once belonged to the great Fiorello La Guardia himself. There, I flipped the pages of my daily calendar to see how my week looked. Jammed, as usual, although with some juggling, I could possibly manage to eke out a few spare hours or so tomorrow.

The third thing I did was reach for the phone with one hand and my Rolodex with the other. I efficiently looked up and dialed the number of Sebastian Nicolay's law firm in Bergen County. With any luck at all, he, like me, would be the type who got in and rolled up his sleeves early every morning.

I was in luck, as it turned out. After I'd told her who I was, his secretary informed me that he was, indeed, available, and would be right with me.

A moment later, Nicolay was saying, "Ed, how are you?"

"I'm fine, Sebastian—wanted to offer my condolences to you and your wife on the loss of her godson," I told him sincerely. "Saturday night must have been quite an ordeal for you."

"It was," he said somberly. "I don't know how poor Tetty is ever going to get over what happened. She's been distraught. I hated to leave her this morning, but I'm very busy today. We're leaving next weekend for Africa—Tetty's always wanted to go, and I promised I'd take her this year for our twenty-fifth anniversary—and I have a lot of loose ends to tie up now."

"I can imagine." I paused to sip some coffee, then asked cautiously, "I don't suppose the police have found out who did it?"

He confirmed what I already knew, having read the morning papers in the limo on the way to work.

"No, they haven't, Ed. They're working on it, but so far, they haven't come up with anything. At least, they hadn't as of last night. Tetty and I spoke to a detective friend of yours, Charley Deacon, late last evening. He drove out to our place."

I nodded. I'd tried to reach Charley last night, to no avail. I'd been planning to have him update me on the case. Not that I expected him to give me any insider information. Charley's strictly a by-the-books detective.

Besides, I didn't think he'd take kindly to my poking my nose into yet another case. Not that he wasn't pleased that I'd solved the Krieg murder, but he wasn't exactly thrilled when the tabloids made noises about the NYPD being too inept to nail the killer on their own.

"He's a nice man," Sebastian went on. "Said he used to be on your bodyguard detail."

"That, he did. Charley's the best. Er, Sebastian . . ." I wondered if I was out of line, but I had to ask. "I don't suppose I could meet with you and Tetty on Tuesday afternoon . . . ?"

"Tomorrow? The funeral is being held in the morning, so I've cleared my calendar for the day. . . ."

I had suspected as much, having read Conor Matthews's obituary. It was at a church in South Orange, where Matthews had grown up.

Sebastian started to add tentatively, "But—"

"I had planned to attend the funeral," I interrupted hurriedly. "Let me take you and Tetty out to lunch after the service. It will be good for you two to get away from everything for a little while . . . unless you have other family obligations?"

"No," Sebastian said. "Conor didn't have much family. His mother's been dead for years, his father's not in the picture, and he was an only child. The arrangements are being handled by his fiancée. Tetty and I have never even met her, though I imagine we'll see her at the wake this evening."

"That would be Kellie Farrell?"

"His costar in the show, yes. Poor thing. Whenever I remember how she sat there on the stage, cradling Conor in her lap, screaming for help . . ."

He trailed off.

Resisting the urge to ask what he knew about their relationship, I said sympathetically, "I know. It must have been very difficult for her."

"Must have been. Not that she hasn't managed to pull herself together since, according to a friend of Tetty's, who works as a receptionist at the Blessed Sacrament—that's the church where the funeral will be held."

Did I detect a note of irony in his voice?

Before I could ask, I heard a faint ringing tone and Sebastian said, "There's my secretary on the intercom, Ed. I'm expecting a call from the District Attorney's office. Shall we meet tomorrow, then?"

"I'll see you there," I agreed.

After hanging up, I decided I would have Maria arrange for one of my aides to find out what time and where the funeral would be held, and make transportation arrangements.

As for juggling my schedule—well, Maria could take care of that for me. She had a wonderful knack for being no-nonsense, yet charming. It came in handy whenever I had to let someone down, which was more often than I'd have liked.

Tomorrow, it would be Carmine Bello, one of my deputy mayors, with whom I was supposed to discuss the strained budget. He'd be glad to postpone that meeting, I was sure, since he had quite a bit of explaining to do. So I didn't feel the least bit guilty backing out.

And as for my lunch with my press secretary—that, too, could wait. I was supposed to be taking her out to belatedly celebrate her birthday, which had been on Flag Day. Another few days' delay would hardly throw her—especially under the circumstances. Matthews's funeral was undoubtedly going to be a high-profile affair, and it's always good for me to put in an appearance when it comes to that sort of thing.

"Mr. Mayor?" Maria appeared in the doorway. "Your first appointment is here."

"Wonderful. Send them into the Blue Room."

A minute later, a group of disgruntled union representatives began hurling their list of complaints at me, and another work week had begun.

FOUR

I managed to track down Charlie Deacon on Monday afternoon with a phone call to his apartment in St. Albans out in Queens. He sounded happy to hear from me.

"How's the Matthews case going?" I asked after we'd exchanged the usual pleasantries.

"Now why did I suspect you might be calling about that?" he asked, sounding amused. "To tell you the truth, I'm not officially working on the case. It's Rabinowitz and Swanson's deal, although I've been assisting with it. Everything is status quo, as I'm sure you read in this morning's papers. And I can't discuss it in much detail, as I'm sure you know by now, Mayor."

What did I tell you? Charley follows the rules—not that there's anything wrong with that.

"Listen, Charley, between you and me, I'm planning to do some digging around, see what I can come up with," I told him. "I have some connections in the theater business who might be more willing to talk to me than they would to the police . . . no offense."

"None taken. Don't think I don't know that the NYPD isn't exactly on anyone's list of favorites these days. First the scandal with that S.O.B. Brooks—who, last I heard, had moved out of town. If he hadn't, I'd have run him out. Then we had that little incident on Stratford Avenue . . ."

"Yeah, I know," I said, aware that he was referring to the tragic foul-up in which a rookie had accidentally shot and wounded an innocent street kid while chasing an armed robber in the South Bronx last month.

"Charley," I said, "can you tell me what you've got so far in the Matthews case?"

He hesitated. "You know I can't—"

"I'm not asking for top secret info here, Charley. Just give me the facts."

"The facts? It's just like the papers are saying, Mayor. We've got hundreds of witnesses to the murder itself—some of the most elite residents of this city. But no one knows how those bullets got into the gun. We've been questioning the actors—"

"Kellie Farrell and Wesley Fisk?" I cut in.

"Yes. Neither of whom, I might add, is particularly cooperative."

"Well, she just lost her fiancé," I pointed out. "You'd have to expect her to be upset. And he's the one who did the shooting, so he's got to be distraught."

"You'd think so, wouldn't you?"

"What do you mean?" I asked, intrigued.

"Only that he's about as emotional as the stone lions in front of the public library," Charley said. "And Kellie Farrell's the opposite—she gets hysterical every time we try to talk to her."

"Like I said . . ."

"I know," Charley told me. "She's grieving. We'll give her some time, but she'd better get her act together and tell us what, if anything, she knows."

I changed the subject. "What about fingerprints?"

"We're looking into that, of course. Trouble is, quite a few people have handled the gun in the course of performances. We're not counting on fingerprints to offer anything conclusive, though you never know."

"Who had access to the gun?"

"We've talked to Teresa Jaffe, the stage manager, and Dan Marinowski, the propertyman for the production. Both say the gun is kept under strict guard, locked into a prop cabinet. The two of them supposedly had the only keys. But with all the chaos backstage during the performances, it isn't hard to imagine someone having an opportunity to tamper with it. Again, we're looking into it."

"What's your theory, Charley? Off the record, of course."

"That it was someone closely connected with the show," he said, after hedging for a moment. "Someone who knew the theater and the actors' routines. Someone who had a reason to want Matthews dead."

I nodded. "Any official suspects?"

"Officially, no. Again, off the record—and this is just between you and me—we're looking closely at Farrell and Fisk."

"Anyone else?"

"I'll let you know. I've got to run now, Mayor. Selma's calling me for lunch, and then I've got to get to the subway and get to work."

"Okay, Charley. Thanks for filling me in."

"Anytime. You helped us out last time—maybe you can do it again. But if I were you, I wouldn't tell too many people. We don't want it getting out, if you know what I mean. It wouldn't look great for the force."

"Right. My lips are sealed, Charley."

Dinner at Cafe Animale is always an experience.

The small, eclectic restaurant is located a block from the apartment I still keep on Washington Place in the Village. My reasons for choosing to meet Sybil there were threefold:

One: I wanted to stop at my old apartment to pick up the soundtrack CD for *The Last Laugh,* as well as a collection of old *Playbills* I'd accumulated over the years. I thought they might yield something interesting about Conor Matthews or one of the others involved in the case.

Two: I'd succumbed to a hot pastrami on rye at lunch this afternoon. I couldn't help it. I had a lunch meeting at the best deli in the city—what was I supposed to order? Tuna salad? Hardly. So for dinner, I would make up for it by having something healthy. And since Cafe Animale has an all-vegetarian menu, I figured I could avoid temptation.

Three: The place is one of the noisiest restaurants in the city. I figured there was no chance that anyone would overhear my conversation with Sybil, even if they tried. And believe me, when you're mayor of New York, people are always doing their best to eavesdrop. The last thing I wanted was for the public to get wind that I was investigating another homicide.

Sybil was late, as usual.

I sat and sipped an iced herbal tea while I waited. I certainly wasn't bored.

First of all, people kept coming up to me to chat. It's a good thing I enjoy making small talk most of the time, because wherever I go, I'm invariably recognized and approached.

This evening, I had the pleasure of discussing virtues and drawbacks of bus-shelter advertisements with an earnest young Madison Avenue exec, followed by a highly political but not antagonistic conversation with a group of long-haired NYU students. That discussion was interrupted by a grandmother who had lived off Pelham Parkway for eighty years and wanted me to autograph napkins for all her neighbors. On her heels came two towering Swedish au pairs who told me, in charming English, how much they loved living in New York.

"So do I," I assured them. "I wouldn't live anywhere else in the world." They took turns shaking my hand profusely before returning to their vegetarian nachos.

When I wasn't engaged in social interaction, I was admiring my surroundings.

The walls of the cafe are painted in a mural that represents an African plain, with various animals depicted in broad, almost cartoonish style. Rather than music, the stereo system continually plays a jungle sound-effects tape that captures chirping birds and chattering chimps. The floors are zebra-striped, the chairs covered in fake leopard-skin upholstery, and the waiters and waitresses are outfitted as various furry and feathered friends.

By the time Sybil swept into the restaurant, I had counted a rabbit, a dog, a lion, and a kangaroo among tonight's staff.

"Sorry I'm late, Ed," she said, pecking me on the cheek and slipping into the chair I'd pulled out for her. She was wearing a tailored blue dress and sensible-looking pumps—but her earrings consisted of miniature plastic football helmets emblazoned with the New York Giants' logo.

"Stuck in traffic?" I inquired. I knew there'd been a water main break on the Upper West Side, but I'd been told that was cleared up late this afternoon.

"Nope," Sybil said breezily. "I wanted to watch the tail end of the early newscast. They were interviewing the team about tonight's game."

"What did the players say?" I asked. As mayor, I naturally have an interest, if not the time, to follow our local teams as closely as Sybil does.

"That they're going to annihilate the Saints—what else?" Sybil shrugged. "And they'd better do just that. I've already announced, in my column, that I have a gut feeling this is going to be a sterling season for the Giants."

"Let's hope so."

Our waiter—a young man who sported a perpetual smirk, a crew cut, and a curious mosaic pattern painted on his face—appeared and took Sybil's drink order. She went with fresh carrot-parsley juice, which surprised me, since she never was much of a health nut. In fact, she'd grumbled when I'd suggested the Cafe Animale.

"I'm in an adventurous mood," she informed me when I questioned her about her choice.

"In that case, why don't you ask our waiter what he's supposed to be. I haven't been able to figure it out."

"You can't be serious, Ed. He's a snake."

I blinked. "A snake?"

"What else?" She shook her head and clucked her tongue at me. "I must say, I'm having second thoughts about your powers of detection, my dear Mr. Mayor. How are you going to figure out who killed Conor Matthews if you can't even solve the mystery of our waiter's reptilian costume?"

"Will you keep your voice down, please, Sybil?" I asked—not that there was the least chance anyone could hear us over the roar of a lion, courtesy of the cafe's sound system.

She merely rolled her eyes, propped her elbows on the table, and said, "Well?"

"Well, what?"

"Well, have you come up with any leads yet?"

"Not yet. That's what I need you for. Tell me everything you know about Conor Matthews."

She didn't bat an eye. "He's from Jersey," she announced promptly. "An only child. His father, Richard, was an accountant, one of those mild-mannered types who suddenly cracks. Maybe a midlife crisis—he was a lot older than his wife. In any case, he started cheating and took off with some bimbo when Conor was just a kid, about three or four, I think."

"That's tough."

"You bet. His wife lost it after he left. She'd always been a drinker, but she went overboard after the divorce. Conor used to find her passed out on the floor when he came home from school."

She paused and wrinkled her nose in distaste as the waiter set a tall glass of drab-colored juice in front of her.

"Can I take your orders, Mr. Mayor?" he asked, a little too impatiently for my taste. There was something about him that I didn't like, and I told myself that it had nothing to do with the fact that he was dressed as a snake.

"We haven't looked at the menus yet," I told him. "Sorry. Give us a few minutes."

"Of course." With a brisk nod, he slithered away to wait on a couple who were clearly advocates of body piercing.

I forced my eyes away from the hoop earring jutting from the woman's upper lip and glanced down at my menu.

"I'm going with the veggie stir-fry," I decided. "How about you?"

"The tofu salad sounds good," Sybil ventured. "Although what I really want is a cheeseburger—bloody rare, with cajun fries on the side. And a tall, frosty beer."

For someone who's so outdoorsy and athletic, the woman has some surprisingly unhealthy habits.

"You shouldn't eat ground beef that isn't fully cooked," I chided her, even though my mouth was watering at the thought of it.

"There are a lot of things I shouldn't do," Sybil informed me, arching a plucked brow. "But if I didn't, life wouldn't be much fun. Now, where were we?"

"Matthews's mother was passed out after school . . ."

"Oh, right. Anyway, the woman drank herself to death by the time she was forty."

I nodded. Tetty Nicolay had told me she'd died young. "How old was Conor then?" I asked.

"I think he was a freshman in college. Her death left him with no one. Thanks to his bitter mother, he'd grown up hating his father, who had a new family by that time with his second wife anyway."

"What about the Nicolays? Tetty told me Conor and his mother rented the guest house on their property. I thought he was close to them."

She shrugged. "I got the impression he was a real loner. But you'll have to ask your friend Tetty about that."

"Can I ask you something, Sybil?"

"Feel free."

"How do you know all these details?"

"I interviewed Matthews for the *Register* when he took over the Quincy Tate role."

"And he told you about his cheating father and his drunken mother?"

Sybil shrugged. "He told me some of it, implied the rest. Let me tell you something, Ed. Conor Matthews was a notorious teetotaler. Vehemently antialcohol, antidrug. He was known for putting a damper on cast parties—I'd heard he used to lecture people on the evils of drinking, that sort of thing. When I asked him about it, he said it was because of his mother's problem."

Our waiter showed up again, pad in hand. "Ready to order yet?"

We were, and did. He seemed to linger an extra long time, refilling our water glasses and brushing nonexistent crumbs off the table. I got the impression he was interested in what we were saying, and wondered if he'd overheard anything.

Annoyed, I gave him the brow. He got the message and vanished.

As soon as we were alone again, I asked Sybil to continue with her story.

"I'll save you listening to me droning on about the basics, like about where he went to school and who he studied acting with," she said. "I'll fax you my article on Matthews as soon as I get to the office tomorrow morning."

"Fine. Now tell me what you didn't write about in the paper."

"He wasn't very likeable," she said without missing a beat.

"Matthews?"

"Who else?" Sybil sipped her drink and made a face. "In fact, he was about as appealing as this juice. Bland, yet with an underlying bitterness."

I allowed her a moment to be pleased with her own clever analogy, then said, "Elaborate, please."

"He had one of those expressionless voices, almost a monotone, and he droned on about his roles in classical productions. Shakespeare this, Shakespeare that. It was all I could do not to yawn."

"All actors like to talk about their credits."

"I know. It wasn't that, it was just . . . he seemed to want to play up his Shakespeare stuff, almost as though he were ashamed of doing a big, splashy, commercial show like *The Last Laugh*. And he maintained an emotional distance that I don't often encounter when I speak with performers."

"Interesting."

"He was definitely bitter about the fact that his opening-night reviews for *The Last Laugh* weren't great. They compared him to Beau Walton—"

"That was to be expected," I interjected, and she nodded.

"Of course it was," Sybil went on, "but he seemed somewhat bitter at Nolan MacDougall, too. I think he felt that MacDougall could have done something to remedy the bad publicity the show was getting after Beau Walton left."

"But by that time, MacDougall was wrapped up in his own problems," I pointed out. "The lawsuit hit the fan right after Matthews started, didn't it?"

"Absolutely. And I think part of it was that MacDougall never wanted Walton to leave the show, and everyone knew it—including Matthews. Conor had his big break—the lead in a huge show, something every actor lives for. But he seemed to look down his nose at fluffy, crowd-pleasing theater, and I got the feeling he felt compromised having sacrificed his principles for a shot at stardom. Not that it mattered."

"Because . . . ?"

"He was second fiddle, anyway, because of Walton's enormous popularity. And the show went downhill right after Matthews took over. It had been sold out on weekends for almost ten years straight, and suddenly, scads of tickets were available at the discount booth on Broadway. Although that situation's undoubtedly going to do an about-face after what happened on Saturday. Did you hear that as of today, the box office reports that tickets are selling faster than fresh hot bagels outside Grand Central during the morning rush hour?"

"So I've heard. What about Kellie Farrell? When did Matthews take up with her?"

"Oh, they were an item right from the start," Sybil said. "She'd joined the cast a few weeks before Conor did, so they were in the same boat as newcomers. When I interviewed him, though, he denied having a significant other."

"Did you ask about Kellie?"

"Naturally I asked about her. I'd heard the rumors, of course. And when I mentioned her name casually early in the interview, his eyes lit up. When I came right out and asked him if he was involved with anyone, he told me that yes, he was in love, but he didn't believe in discussing his romantic affairs with reporters. And shortly after that, he called an end to the interview."

"Have you ever met Kellie?"

"No. But word has it that she's something of a cliché. Spoiled. Self-centered. Ambitious."

"What do you think Conor saw in her?"

"I have no idea," Sybil told me. "Though of course, she's a beautiful little thing, with all that long blond hair and those big baby blues. And obviously, he thought the world of her, and she had him fooled. I wouldn't be surprised if she'd played a role in Conor Matthews's death, Ed. She should be your number-one suspect!"

I placed a vertical finger against my lips. "Shh, Sybil. The last thing I need is for someone to overhear and figure out that I'm—"

"Here we are, Mr. Mayor," the snake-waiter said, appearing out of nowhere at my elbow with a tray of food.

As he set our orders before us, I couldn't help but notice a gleam in his eye—one that hadn't been there before.

Something told me that Sybil and I had better curtail our conversation about the murder.

For the rest of the meal, we discussed football and food, and our waiter showed no apparent interest in our conversation.

But the damage had, as I suspected, already been done.

____ FIVE

KAN KOCH KATCH KILLER?

That was the Tuesday morning headline concocted by Sybil's chief rival, Clancy O'Brien, in his column published in the *Manhattan Monitor*, which is the *Register*'s biggest tabloid competitor.

It was Detective David Rabinowitz who alerted me to the news, with a phone call that caught me on my way out the door at Gracie Mansion.

"You trying to do my job, Mr. Mayor?" was his greeting.

"I beg your pardon?"

"According to this morning's *Monitor,* you're playing detective again, trying to solve the Matthews case."

Flabbergasted, I abruptly put him on hold and quickly obtained a copy of the paper from one of my bodyguards. They always have the morning's newspapers waiting for me in the limo, so that I can look through them during my trip downtown.

I snorted and rolled my eyes as I scanned the gossip column, which led with an item that informed readers of "the mayor's top-secret late-night meeting with a Broadway insider" and "hizzoner's plan to once again outdo the fumbling NYPD."

"This is ludicrous," I told Rabinowitz, getting back on the line. "Why would I want to outdo the police department? It's my responsibility to make sure you guys look *good,* not *bad.* "

"Mmm hmm," was all he said.

"Listen, Detective, do you actually believe that I'm sneaking around town in the dead of night, having meetings with Manhattan's version of Deep Throat?"

"I wouldn't be surprised . . ."

"Ridiculous!" I snorted. "I had dinner last night—an *early* dinner—with Sybil Baker. We discussed the Matthews case, yes. But who in New York *isn't* discussing it?"

I had a point, and he said nothing to that. But he did ask me if I had any notion of playing detective again.

"I never 'play' at anything, Rabinowitz," I informed him coolly. "As mayor, I'm much too busy for that. But I am interested in the murder, and if there's anything I can do to help you solve it—"

"We appreciate your offer, Mr. Mayor," he interrupted. "But believe me, we're not 'fumbling' this case."

"I never said you were!" I was getting frustrated, not to mention irritated. You'd think a member of the NYPD would know better than to believe everything he reads. Still, I knew where he was coming from, in a sense.

I tried to regain my control and said reasonably, "Look, Detective, you guys are the finest police force in the world. I'm always the first to say it."

"Then trust us to do our jobs."

Exasperated, I said, "I do trust you. But if there's something I happen to come up with—a clue, or something that might help— well, don't tell me you don't want to know about it!"

There was a moment of silence on the other end of the line. Then he said, "You'd better get moving, Mayor, before rush hour traffic kicks in."

He was right, of course. It isn't easy to get from Gracie Mansion to City Hall in the height of morning traffic.

"Right," I said hurriedly, checking my watch. "But look, just so we're clear on this, I'm *not* trying to stick my nose where it doesn't belong. This city is my business, and I plan to lend a helping hand wherever I can. As mayor, I'd be thrilled to get every lowdown criminal off our streets, including whoever killed Conor Matthews on Saturday night."

"Fine. Do whatever you have to. Just keep quiet about it, will you? Don't make us look bad. That's all I ask. In case you hadn't noticed, the press isn't crazy about us these days. You, they love."

I had to snort at that.

I considered telling him that I hadn't exactly stood in the middle of Times Square and announced that I was investigating the Matthews murder. But then, what would be the point?

It was obvious that as far as Rabinowitz was concerned, I had no business investigating the case. What he didn't understand was that I consider almost everything that affects this city to be my business.

Furthermore, I'm a pragmatic guy, and there was no reason I, along with anyone else who could help, shouldn't do whatever was possible to uncover the truth behind Matthews's murder.

To be perfectly frank, I was determined—well, all right . . .

To Katch a Killer.

When I got to my office, I had three messages from Sybil, as well as the faxed article about Conor Matthews. I put that into my briefcase to read later, then quickly called her back, though the chairman of the Taxi and Limousine Commission was undoubtedly losing patience in the small conference room. Our meeting was already a half hour behind schedule.

"Did you see it?" Sybil asked, after snatching up the phone on the first ring.

"The fax? Yes, thanks."

"Not the fax," she snapped. "The column in the *Monitor.*"

"Of course I saw it."

"That damn snake. He must have sold this tidbit of gossip to O'Brien. Every waiter in Manhattan knows old Clancy's so hard up for material that he's willing to generously compensate eavesdroppers for filling him in on anything they overhear."

"Well, the damage is done," I pointed out. "Listen, I'm late for a—"

"And I'm late for my meeting with my personal trainer," Sybil cut in. "But listen, Ed, you can't expect me to sit back and let Clancy O'Brien go with this scoop while I reveal nothing. You promised me an exclusive about your involvement in the case."

"*After* I've solved it," I reminded her. "Right now, the last thing I want to do is fan the flames. Don't you dare write a single word about this, Sybil."

"But *I'm* the Broadway insider! And anyway, when I made that deal with you, I had no idea that smarmy O'Brien was going to pull the rug out from under me. I have a job to do, Ed."

I snorted at that. "So do I, Sybil. And right now, I'm late for a meeting. Just keep your end of the bargain, and I'll keep mine. A deal's a deal. I have to run."

She was grumbling when I hung up.

I shook my head all the way to the small conference room down the hall. Much as I loved being mayor, there were times when being famous was a colossal inconvenience.

Later that Tuesday morning was *not* one of those times. Quite the contrary, in fact.

Thanks to a broken-down bus, the Lincoln tunnel was a mess. It didn't look like anyone was going to get to New Jersey any time before Christmas.

But my driver made a few calls on the limousine radio, and voila! They opened an emergency lane for the mayoral entourage so that we could zip through.

We made it to the funeral in South Orange with time to spare. In fact, we were among the first to arrive at the Blessed Sacrament Church. The other early-comers were camped out in television news trucks, and they scrambled for their cameras and microphones as soon as I stepped out of the car into the glaring September sun.

"Mr. Mayor, is it true that you're conducting an investigation into the Matthews murder?"

"Do you know who killed Conor Matthews?"

"Why are you here, Mr. Mayor?"

I ignored the questions that bombarded me, not in the mood, under the circumstances, to deliver my usual snappy comebacks. The fact that this was a place of worship did little to restrain the frenzied journalists, but I had no intention of helping them to turn the funeral into a circus.

My bodyguards ushered me through carved double doors and into dim, welcome silence. I spotted the perfect pew—toward the back and on the aisle, at my insistence. I didn't want to be conspicuous, particularly with the press swarming all over the place.

From my seat, I watched the trail of mourners trickle in.

The crowd couldn't have been more disparate. Salt-and-pepper permed middle-aged women crowded alongside long-haired, bearded theatrical techies. Reporters dotted the congregation, deceptively decorous, their cameras and recorders nowhere to be seen—for once. I saw several big-name Broadway stars, as well as lesser-knowns and unknowns. There were producers and directors; dancers and chorus members—all of them subdued and wearing sober expressions.

Conor Matthews's agent, the well-known and flamboyant Artie Masters, sniffled audibly as he took his seat toward the front. He was accompanied by his longtime companion, Dexter Damian, who seemed to be whispering words of comfort as they sat waiting for the service to begin.

Beau Walton came in with Nolan MacDougall; both wore well-cut charcoal summer suits and dark glasses, which neither removed until they were seated.

Sebastian and Tetty Nicolay entered and sat in the second row. He clutched her elbow; she clutched a handkerchief.

When a tall, handsome man with graying temples passed by, I saw, in his profile, a distinct resemblance to Conor Matthews. I frowned slightly and watched him proceed down the aisle. On his arm was a beautiful, well-dressed brunette who couldn't have been a day over thirty. With them were two ponytailed adolescents, both wearing sullen expressions.

When they filed into the front pew, my hunch was confirmed. This would be Matthews's wayward father, Richard, escorted by his second family. He appeared stiff and stared straight ahead, as though he were fully aware that several of the Jersey matrons were whispering among themselves and glancing in his direction.

Just before ten, Kellie Farrell entered. Alone. She wore a simple black dress that hugged her slim figure, along with black patent sling-backs and gold-rimmed designer sunglasses. Her long blond hair was pulled back into a simple ponytail secured by a black bow. In her left hand was a Prada handbag. In her right, a handkerchief and what appeared to be a small teddy bear.

I watched her make her way down the aisle, her head held high, her expression inscrutable. She slid into the first pew across the aisle from Matthews's father just as the white-robed priest, Father Carney, appeared at the altar.

Being a political figure, I have attended more than my share of funerals—some of them dignified state affairs, others heart-wrenching emotional ordeals. This particular one was neither, although Tetty Nicolay, Artie Masters, Kellie Farrell, and a few others made good use of their hankies. Matthews's father was conspicuously dry-eyed, as were Walton and MacDougall, though I observed that all three used handkerchiefs to mop sweat from their foreheads.

The church, one of those old-fashioned Gothic structures, wasn't air-conditioned. The temperature outside was ninety degrees; inside, it had to be over a hundred. Every seat was taken and mourners stood three-deep along the back.

I found myself wondering how many were there to pay their last respects to the deceased, and how many made up the usual conglomeration of snoops, publicity-seekers, and ghouls who showed up whenever someone was murdered in a high-profile case.

The papers yesterday and this morning had been full of grisly particulars about Conor Matthews's death. Eyewitnesses found it necessary to recall, in vivid detail, the spurting blood and the ghastly shrieks of Kellie Farrell. The medical examiner had released autopsy findings, noting that Matthews had died almost instantly of a single bullet wound to the heart. The body had been released to Matthews's fiancée, in the absence of next of kin, for burial, and the case was being investigated by the NYPD.

Though the church was, as I said, filled to capacity, I noted that there were some very prominent no-shows.

Sybil, of course, was one. She was having brunch at the Central Park South duplex of pop music's most elusive and scandal-ridden diva. If it had been anything else, Sybil would have canceled in favor of attending the funeral. However, the star was purportedly about to announce her third divorce, and Sybil was determined to get the scoop.

Wesley Fisk hadn't shown up at Blessed Sacrament, either, much to my surprise. I hadn't expected him to appear at Kellie Farrell's side, but I'd thought that as a fellow cast member, he would at least attend the service.

Hmm . . . very intriguing, I thought, mentally going over again the evidence that had led me to label Fisk a prime suspect. It was substantial. And he had, in fact, pulled the trigger, though that didn't, under these unique circumstances, make him a murderer. Yet if he *was* the culprit, wouldn't he want to at least put on an innocent facade and make like a bereaved friend? On the other hand, his not showing up didn't automatically make him guilty, though I was definitely more suspicious than ever.

I had also expected to see Rabinowitz and Swanson in attendance, but they were nowhere to be found. I later discovered that they were stuck in tunnel traffic, and the service was over by the time the hapless detectives arrived via backtracking to the George Washington Bridge.

I won't admit to being secretly pleased . . . oh, all right, I will admit it. The last thing I wanted that Tuesday morning was David Rabinowitz dogging my heels as I mingled with the other mourners on the steps outside after the service.

Naturally, I was shadowed by my bodyguards, who drew curious glances from the throng. Mohammed and the others were characteristically wary, as though someone were going to take a shot at me here on the threshold of a church, a notion I found unlikely, though not altogether out of the question, I supposed.

The press had been relegated to the street, thanks to Father Carney's intervention. So my interaction with the mourners was relatively free of distractions . . . with the exception of my dutiful greetings to the familiar faces I kept spotting—and the unfamiliar ones who kept spotting me.

"Hey, Ed!" called a young actor type with a hoop earring and a well-scrubbed complexion. "Thanks for the amazing speech! You really gave us your support! We needed you, man, and you came through."

"No problem," I said, as though I knew exactly what he was talking about. As mayor, you find yourself doing that a lot.

I realized, after I had moved on, that he was probably referring to the luncheon I had attended back in July to benefit a fledgling charity organization for Broadway actors suffering from AIDS. The kid was right. I had been brilliant that day, and it was nice someone had noticed.

"Mr. Mayor, can I ask you something?" asked another stranger, a skeleton-thin young woman wearing the thickest eyeliner I've ever seen.

"Why not?" I shrugged, keeping my eye on Tetty and Sebastian, who were caught up in a crowd of their cronies. Sebastian caught my glance and motioned that they'd be with me as soon as they could, and I motioned that they should take their time. In all honesty, the longer they took, the better. It would give me an opportunity to approach both Richard Matthews and Kellie Farrell—once I managed to answer the young lady's question.

"I heard there's a piano in Gracie Mansion," she said. "Did you ever consider hiring someone to play—you know, when you're hosting dinner parties and receptions? Because I'm at Juilliard and I—"

"Actually," I interrupted politely, because it was absolutely necessary, if I was going to get to Farrell and the elder Matthews, "we do have several pianists that we use regularly, but thanks for the offer."

"Here's my card," she said, shoving a small pink rectangle at me.

I dutifully tucked it into the pocket of my suit and thanked her. "Now if you'll excuse me . . ."

I had just spotted Matthews's father, who was wearing a distracted expression that suggested he was going to bolt as soon as he could extract himself from the sympathy-extenders who seemed as awkward as he did. His eyes kept shifting from his wife and daughters, who were clustered impatiently in the background, to a Volvo station wagon that was parked at the curb nearby.

As soon as a blue-haired, black-garbed woman released his sleeve from her manicured grasp, I cornered him. "Mr. Matthews, I presume?"

He turned in dismay, having been on the verge of making his

escape. His eyes widened slightly when he recognized me, and he looked flustered. "Yes, I am," he said.

"I'm Ed Koch."

He nodded and I shook his hand, saying, "I'm terribly sorry for the loss of your son. Please accept my most profound condolences."

"Thank you," he murmured without correcting me, confirming my assumption that he was, indeed, *that* Mr. Matthews.

"It must have been a horrible shock for you."

"Yes . . . it was." He appeared explicitly uncomfortable.

I decided that there was something about him that I didn't like. The man's eyes betrayed an inner core of ice, and he displayed an absence of emotion that one would hardly expect from a bereaved father at his son's funeral.

"I know how proud of your son you must have been," I went on. "Conor was an exceptional actor."

"Yes . . . he was."

"Such a shame . . . he was so promising. I'd say his work in *The Last Laugh* was his best ever, wouldn't you?"

"It was, er—actually, Mr. Mayor, I hadn't had the opportunity to see my son's performance."

I feigned surprise. "You hadn't?"

"I—no. I—Conor and I have been estranged since he was a boy. But I did love him deeply," he quickly tacked on, sounding as programmed as my bank's automated telephone help line, "and I've always wished things could have been different. Not raising him, not seeing him grow up, has been my biggest regret in life."

Yeah, sure it has, I thought. Feeling more sorry than ever for poor dead Conor, I set the pathetic senior Matthews free with another brief word of sympathy. The moment I did, he gratefully dashed off to the Volvo at the curb, the three spoiled-looking females in tow. He practically burned rubber as he drove off down the street.

"Who *was* that, Mr. Mayor?" Lou Sabatino, one of my bodyguards, muttered into my ear. He had been hovering, but not close enough to overhear my conversation with Matthews.

"Believe it or not, that was the father of the deceased."

"No."

"Yep."

Lou let out a low whistle. "Me and my old man don't get along, but you'd never see the day he'd act that way at my funeral. In fact, I don't know anyone who'd act that way at my funeral, except maybe my ex-wife's mother."

"I wish I could say the same," I said, shaking my head.

After all, when you're mayor, you tend to have enemies, whether you deserve them or not. But thankfully, my relationship with my own Pop is intact. The old guy's my biggest fan and supporter. I found myself wistfully thinking of him and Mom. They'd left for a cruise to St. Martin just last week, and shortly after their return, they'd be heading down to their condo in Boca Raton for the winter.

I forced my thoughts back to the issue at hand, which was locating the unfortunate fiancée of Conor Matthews.

As it turned out, Kellie Farrell was easy to spot, despite the fact that she was almost a head shorter than most of the crowd. She was holding court near the doors of the church, surrounded by her somber-looking theatrical cronies. One earnest young man was rubbing her shoulders. Another was lighting the cigarette she held to her lips with her right hand, while her left still clutched her handbag and a small furry object.

I made my way over as she exhaled a long stream of smoke through her nostrils.

"Ms. Farrell?" I asked, as the crowd parted, as crowds tend to do, for me and my bodyguards.

She glanced up. She wore sunglasses, masking her eyes, but something about her attitude told me they'd probably lit up when she realized the mayor knew her by name.

"Hello, Mayor," she said, stepping forward to separate herself from her friends. She didn't have a hand to offer, what with the cigarette and all. I saw that it was, indeed, a small brown teddy bear she was holding, rather conspicuously, in fact.

"I just wanted to offer my sympathy on the death of your . . . fiancé," I told her. If she noticed that I missed a beat before labeling Matthews, she didn't let on. I wondered if she was aware that her secret affair with Wesley Fisk wasn't much of a secret.

"Thank you for your kindness," she said graciously.

She was practically waving the teddy bear in my face, so I had to ask about it.

"This?" she asked, as if she were surprised I'd noticed it. She's some actress. "Conor gave it to me after our first date," she said. "I've always treasured it." Her voice broke and she clutched the bear to her heart.

I murmured something appropriate and waited for her to collect herself. She did, and rather quickly.

"I hope you don't mind my smoking," she said, taking a drag, "but I've been an emotional wreck ever since—well, you know. I'd been trying to quit, but I've gone back up to over a pack a day."

I nodded and told her it was quite all right. "Conor's death must have been quite a shock to you," I pointed out, wishing I could see her eyes.

"It was. It was a shock to all of us," she said, gesturing at the cast and crew members who hovered protectively nearby. "Everyone has been just wonderful, helping me through this. Some people think I should take some time off from the show, but believe me, I have no intention of doing that. My best therapy will be in performing. Conor would have wanted the show to go on."

"What about his role?" I asked. "What's going on with his role?"

"As you probably know, Sunday's performances were canceled, and on Mondays, the theater is dark anyway. So luckily, there's been a little time for everyone to catch their breaths. Conor's understudy, Jonathan Patrelli, will take over when we do tonight's performance," she said. "It won't be easy for him, either, though. He was Conor's closest friend—he's the one who delivered the eulogy."

I nodded, remembering the solemn, handsome young man who had taken the podium during the service. His words had been brief, reminding the congregation of Conor Matthews's talent, saying that the world would sorely miss someone who might have become one of the greatest actors of all time. He had ended with a quote from Conor's favorite play, Shakespeare's *Othello:*

Who can control his fate? 'Tis not so now.
Be not afraid . . .
Here is my journey's end.

I supposed the quote was fitting out of context, as it mentioned fate and death. As a fan of Shakespeare myself, I knew the lines had been lifted from the final scene in the tragedy, where Othello is about to plunge his sword into his own chest and end his misery. Patrelli had dropped the inappropriate line *though you do see me weaponed* in order to make it fit.

"I hope you don't mind my asking," Kellie Farrell was saying, "but I heard you were investigating Conor's death. Is that true?"

"I would like to see the killer caught, yes," I said carefully. "But I'm not a member of the NYPD, and I don't pretend to be."

"Of course you don't. Who'd want to be associated with such a bunch of—sorry," she interrupted herself and clamped her mouth shut.

"What were you going to say?" I asked, aware that Mohammed and Lou, NYPD officers both, were bristling beside me.

"Nothing. It's just . . . those detectives won't leave me alone, and I can't tolerate their attitudes."

"What detectives?"

"Their names are Rabinowitz and Swanson," she said, cordially exhaling another stream of smoke to the side, so it wouldn't hit me in the face. "He's a fat slob, and someone should tell *her* that she'd look much better with her hair styled differently. She goes around looking like a Gestapo warden or something. And there's another one, Charley Deacon. The three of them have been all over me since Saturday night, asking ridiculous questions. I have no intention of telling any of them anything. Don't they know I'm in mourning?"

"I think it would be wise for you to cooperate with the police, Ms. Farrell," I said pointedly. "They're only trying to find out who murdered your fiancé."

"No, they're trying to pin it on me," she burst out with surprising vehemence. "And believe me, Mr. Mayor, I will sue this city if they dare accuse me of murdering Conor. My career will be destroyed. I was going to marry the man, for God's sake. I had absolutely nothing to do with his death. And neither did Wesley Fisk," she added impulsively, then promptly looked as though she wished she hadn't brought him up.

I nodded, thinking that if I kept silent, she'd have to keep talking and perhaps reveal more about her relationship with Wesley.

I was wrong.

She hesitated a moment, then glanced around and leaned closer to me. "I'd like to talk to you, Mayor," she said in a low voice. "Privately."

"About the case?"

She nodded. "Can we meet for lunch this week?"

I happened to know that I hadn't scheduled a lunch meeting for Thursday. I like to keep at least one day a week free, so that I can order Chinese or deli takeout and eat at my desk, working straight through. You wouldn't believe the amount of paper that stacks up when you're mayor, and there are days when you just have to shut yourself away and spend several hours getting it under control.

I told Kellie Farrell that she could meet me at City Hall for lunch on Thursday. "We can eat in, to ensure privacy, if you like," I told her.

"Oh . . ." She looked taken aback. "Actually, I thought we might meet at a restaurant—maybe Le Cirque? I've read that you lunch there on occasion."

I blinked. Lunch at Le Cirque isn't exactly low profile. Then I realized that was exactly what Kellie Farrell was thinking.

Hmm.

Though I was reluctant to risk having the press pick up on my meeting with this particular femme fatale, I decided to play her game. After all, the entire city had already been told I was looking into the case. And I was beginning to think that observing the fair Ms. Farrell's behavior in public would quite possibly be more telling than anything she could reveal to me in private.

"I always enjoy Le Cirque," I told Kellie. "That would be fine. I'll make a reservation for one, and meet you there."

Her face lit up. "Great. I'll be there."

I noticed Sebastian and Tetty approaching.

"Oh," Kellie muttered, "here they come."

"Who?"

"Conor's godmother and her husband. I don't think they like me." She dropped her cigarette onto the cement and ground it out with her heel.

"What makes you say that?" I asked, thinking that Father Carney wouldn't be thrilled to find a cigarette butt on the steps of his church.

"I met them at the wake, and I just got that feeling. I don't think they were pleased that I was the one who was making the funeral arrangements for Conor. But who else did he have?"

She did an abrupt about-face then, and said solemnly, "Mr. and Mrs. Nicolay, how are you holding up?" There was no indication that she felt the least bit uncomfortable in their presence.

Tetty, who appeared emotionally drained, said, "It's been a difficult morning, but that's to be expected. I should ask you how you're doing, dear."

"As well as can be expected," Kellie said, her shoulders slumped. She suddenly sounded as though she were on the verge of tears.

I found myself thinking that perhaps I had misjudged her—maybe she really was nearly overcome with grief. But then I reminded myself that the woman was an actress—possibly one of the best I've ever encountered.

Tetty reached out and patted Kellie's shoulder, and Sebastian cleared his throat and looked at me. "Should we be going, Ed?"

Kellie looked up in surprise, as though it hadn't occurred to her that the Nicolays might be acquaintances of mine.

I agreed that we had better head out, and the three of us exchanged polite farewells with Ms. Farrell. She didn't, I noticed, mention our lunch at Le Cirque in front of the Nicolays. I followed her lead and simply said goodbye, then headed off to my car with Tetty and Sebastian in tow.

SIX

Having lived in Newark for ten years as a boy, I'm fairly familiar with the city, though New York is, of course, my home. I'm partial to a charming little Italian restaurant in Fort Lee, and that was where I took the Nicolays after the funeral.

It's called Ciao Bella, and there, you can get the tastiest plate of spaghetti west of Little Italy. The place smacks of Mediterranean charm, from the vintage wine bottles lining a high shelf in the candlelit dining room, to the small round tables covered in red-and-white-checked oilcloth.

We got there at the height of lunch hour, and the restaurant was jammed with office workers. Most of them recognized Sebastian, who had, after all, been a high-profile congressman in his day. And all of them recognized me, which meant that it was quite a while before we were able to tear ourselves away from the usual round of greetings and small talk.

Finally, we were settled at the back of the dim, air-conditioned room at a cozy table for three, with glasses of Chianti and a basket of flour-dusted rolls in front of us. We'd all ordered today's pasta special, a combination of ham, shrimp, and bacon in a red sauce, served over penne.

Tetty leaned back after the waiter left, took a sip from her glass, and closed her eyes briefly.

"Are you all right?" I asked, reaching out to pat her hand.

"I'm fine," she said, and added, "now. I had been dreading the funeral, and it's over."

"It's never easy to say goodbye to someone," I said, belatedly realizing that I sounded like a Hallmark sympathy card.

"Especially when the person responsible for that someone's death is pretending to grieve along with the rest of us," Tetty said bitterly.

I raised a brow at that and waited for her to continue.

But as she opened her mouth to go on, Sebastian cut her off with a terse, "Be quiet. It's over, Tetty."

"The funeral may be over, but that woman is still going to be seen by everyone as Conor's poor bereaved fiancée."

"Kellie Farrell?" I stated the obvious, in order to jump into the conversation.

They both nodded.

"You think she's the one who loaded real bullets into that gun?" I asked. "What makes you say that?"

"We didn't," Sebastian said quickly, giving Tetty a look.

"Relax, Sebby, this is Ed. We can tell him what we think, and maybe he can do something about it."

He hesitated. Then, apparently fortified by another drink of Chianti, he nodded.

She looked me in the eye and said, "I'd be willing to bet my life on the fact that my godson was murdered by that woman."

"Why?" I asked—not that I would be surprised if I wound up drawing the same conclusion myself.

"She didn't love him. In fact, she was seeing another man behind his back. Wesley Fisk," she added, even as his name echoed in my head.

"How do you know that?" I asked.

"They were both at the wake Monday night," Sebastian said. "They made a big point of arriving and departing separately, but it would have been obvious that there was something going on between them, even if we hadn't found out for sure. The way they looked at each other—well, you couldn't miss their sappy expressions."

"But how did you find out for sure?" I prodded.

Tetty glanced around, as though expecting to find someone listening in. But one of the wonderful things about Ciao Bella is that the tables are spaced for privacy, and the background violin music makes it impossible to eavesdrop.

Still, Tetty leaned forward and lowered her voice as she confided, "Janey Mahler—she's an old friend of mine and she knew Mindy, Conor's mother—anyway, she came to the wake to pay her respects to Conor. She lost a gold earring in the parking lot behind the funeral home when she left, and realized it in the car on her way home. She drove back to find it and was on her hands and knees in the dark between the cars when she happened to hear a conversation between two people."

"Kellie Farrell and Wesley Fisk," Sebastian interjected, and Tetty nodded.

"They had apparently snuck outside to steal a few kisses," Tetty went on bitterly. "And they were talking about Conor's death. They sounded worried, according to Janey. Kellie said something about the police planning to pin a murder charge on her, and Wesley was telling her not to worry, that no one was on to them."

"That certainly is interesting," I said, hardly surprised. "I don't suppose you'd mind if I contacted your friend Janey myself?"

Sebby put in, "She told you in confidence, Tetty. She'd be upset if she knew you'd blabbed it to anyone."

"This is Ed," Tetty said again. "He's not just anyone. He's the mayor. He can help get those murderers into jail."

"If they are murderers," I put in hastily. "We don't have proof of anything."

"No, we certainly don't," Sebastian agreed. He was, after all, a lawyer, and knew better than anyone that it wasn't going to be easy to find evidence against Kellie and Wesley—if they were the guilty parties.

But who else would do it? I found myself thinking.

Then I thought back to my initial list of four suspects. In addition to Farrell and Fisk, I had considered two others.

Beau Walton.

Nolan MacDougall.

"I'd really like to talk to your friend, Tetty," I said, turning my attention back to the matter at hand.

"All right," she said, reaching under the table for her handbag and pulling out a pen and paper. "But don't call her until tomorrow. I'll explain it to her first, so that she won't be angry with me."

I agreed to that, slipped Janey Mahler's number into the pocket of my suit, and concentrated on the plate of steaming pasta the waiter placed in front of me.

Before our lunch ended, Tetty Nicolay had filled me in on Conor Matthews's past, revealing the same hard-luck story Sybil had told me.

She, too, stressed Conor's love of classical theater, and I got the impression that he had, as Sybil hinted, looked down his nose at modern audience-pleasing productions.

I asked her how and when Conor and his mother came to live in their guest house. She said it was a few years after Conor's father had left them. They were destitute—apparently, the deadbeat wasn't paying child support or alimony—and had nowhere else to go. The Nicolays had invited them to move in until they got back on their feet.

I surmised, from the way they talked, that they hadn't charged Mindy Matthews rent for the place, and that they hadn't expected her and Conor to stay for years. But I knew that the Nicolays were charitable people, and I couldn't imagine them throwing a destitute single mother and a fatherless child out on the street.

They'd never had children of their own, which was a shame because they would have made ideal parents, and they live on a sprawling piece of wooded property that would be a great place to grow up. I'd been there once, years ago, for a party.

They told me how, when Conor was younger, Sebby had built him a tree house—an elaborate structure that had a porch and even a little mailbox. They said Conor spent most of his time up there, and that he and his mother had a close relationship until he hit his teens. "She used to climb up the ladder while he was at school and leave little notes for him in his mailbox," they said. "Whenever she did, she'd push the little flag up so that he'd know he had a letter. It was charming."

Tetty told me that his mother had, as Sybil had said, died a few weeks into Conor's first semester in college. He'd gotten a partial scholarship to Ryder College and was planning to earn the rest of his keep as a bookstore clerk. But he dropped out that first January with only one semester under his belt, and never went back.

"We told him he could stay in the guest house as long as he wanted," Tetty said. "But I think it had too many memories for him."

Instead, he rented a one-room apartment in a Manhattan tenement and worked as a word processing temp by day, and as an usher at Broadway theaters by night, so that he could see the productions he would never be able to afford. He had sworn that one day, he would be up on stage as a star, Tetty said.

I was familiar with this classic rags-to-riches aspect of Matthews's story.

But Tetty added some new details—perhaps things Matthews had been reluctant to tell an interviewer. For instance, she said that there was a history of alcoholism in Matthews's family, on his mother's side. And that Matthews himself had been suspended from high school once for showing up drunk. After that, Mindy got him into a local rehab program and he'd purportedly been cured. Indeed, Tetty reiterated Sybil's claim that Matthews was a complete teetotaler; that he was almost preachy about the evils of alcohol.

"At least, that was what I'd heard," she said. "We haven't seen much of Conor over the years. Sebby and I have done our best to stay in touch, but—"

"Let's face it, Tetty," Sebastian had interrupted. "The boy pretty much wrote us off until last week."

"Last week?" I'd asked.

They told me he'd suddenly shown up at their house one stormy night. He'd given them tickets to the gala performance, then asked if he could take a look at the guest house, "for old times' sake."

The Nicolays had given him the keys and left him alone, assuming he needed some private time to reflect on his mother. They said he was gone quite a while before coming back to the main house. When he did, he'd seemed subdued and had left shortly afterward.

"You could just tell he was still grieving, poor thing," Tetty had told me.

She was, not surprisingly, softer on Mindy than Sybil had been.

Tetty portrayed her not as a pathetic lush, but as the victim of a callous man. Having met Richard Matthews, I didn't have a hard time imagining him as the cold, insensitive husband and father Tetty described.

According to her, Mindy had been orphaned young and had married him out of insecurity. She had been a beautiful woman before booze robbed her of her looks, and her utter dependence on her husband had been attractive to a domineering man like Richard Matthews . . . at first.

Tetty sadly and painstakingly described the breakdown of the Matthews family, a story that was heartbreakingly similar to so many others I've heard—the husband who faces a midlife crisis and leaves his wife for a younger woman, the abandoned wife who's left with a child to raise, no marketable skills, and a mountain of bills, and the child who grows up under the shadow of a bitter, lonely mother and a father he never sees.

I felt sorry for Conor Matthews, and wondered whether, if his family life had been different, he'd still be alive today somehow.

As my limo headed across the George Washington Bridge back to Manhattan, I resolved, with more determination than ever, to find out why he wasn't—and who was responsible.

And anyone who knows me will tell you that once Ed Koch decides to do something, he does it . . . and not halfway, either.

I had some people to see—and Janey Mahler and Kellie Farrell were only the first on a long list.

Wednesday morning, the heat and humidity broke for the first time in over a week. The city air was pleasantly cool and dry when I stepped outside Gracie Mansion, and even the cloudy sky was a welcome change. I found myself anticipating autumn—one of my favorite seasons in New York. There's nothing more pleasant than strolling through Central Park on a crisp October afternoon, perhaps stopping for a bag of roasted chestnuts from one of the vendors at the entrance on Fifth Avenue and Fifty-ninth Street.

I was in a contented mood as my limo headed downtown via Second Avenue. The pressures of being mayor and the questions surrounding the Matthews murder seemed far away for that brief interlude.

Then I arrived at City Hall, and all hell broke loose. The sanitation workers were starting to make noises about a strike, a seven-year-old had been shot in a public school in Staten Island, and there had been a deadly apartment building fire in Washington Heights, with some residents claiming the city fire department hadn't gotten there soon enough.

By the time I had dealt with various officials from the sanitation workers' union, the school board, and the fire department, it was noon. I still hadn't had a chance to even think about Conor Matthews, and it looked as though I wouldn't get one. I had a luncheon with the Housing Authority, and immediately after that, I rushed out to Whitestone in Queens to dedicate a memorial plaque in memory of an NYPD officer killed during a hostage situation at a local high school.

My afternoon was filled with meetings and more meetings, and I didn't have a breather until seven o'clock Wednesday evening. That was when I finally had the chance to look through the telephone messages that had accumulated over the course of the day.

Two were of particular interest.

One was from Tetty Nicolay, and my secretary had scrawled, *okay to call J. Mahler now* on the pink slip.

The other was from Nolan MacDougall.

It wasn't until I was ensconced in my home office back at Gracie Mansion that I sat down to return the calls. Only there did I feel that my privacy was ensured. Besides, much as I love my City Hall office, I couldn't stand being cooped up there for another minute. It had been a terminally long day.

Janey Mahler's phone was answered by a teenaged girl—at least, I assumed she was a teenager, by her gum-snapping and the way she giggled when I told her my name.

"Hang on," she said, dropping the phone with a clatter. Then I heard her shrieking, "Mom! Mayor Koch is on the phone for you!"

When Janey Mahler finally picked up the receiver, she sounded subdued.

"I understand Tetty Nicolay told you I was interested in what you have to say about the Matthews murder, Ms. Mahler," I said, businesslike but gentle enough not to scare her off.

"Yes," she said hesitantly. "I really don't know much of anything, but . . ."

"You overheard a conversation between Kelly Farrell and Wesley Fisk."

"Yes."

"Did you see their faces?"

"Not hers. But I peeked to see who she was talking to, once I realized what they were talking about. It was him."

"And what, exactly, did they say?"

"Exactly?" She sounded dubious.

"As close as you can get."

"Okay. She told him she was glad he'd shown up, that she hadn't been sure he was going to. He said he'd come for her sake, and to make things look good."

"He said that? In those words?"

"Yes," she said firmly. "He said, 'I thought it would make things look good if I showed.' "

I jotted a note on my desk pad and said, "Go on."

"She said that a bunch of detectives had been bugging her, asking her questions about her relationship with Conor. She said they didn't seem to believe her when she'd told them she had nothing to do with it. She told Wesley he'd better watch his back, and he told her the detectives had been at his place, too, asking the same questions."

Obviously, I wasn't the only one who had labeled Kellie Farrell and Wesley Fisk the top suspects in the case.

"They kept stopping to kiss," Janey Mahler went on, sounding disgusted. "I could hear them. It wasn't just friendly pecks on the cheek, either. They were real romantic, and their voices were hushed. It seemed a shame, with poor dead Conor just a few feet away, inside, in his coffin."

I murmured that it certainly was a shame, and asked, "What else did they say?"

"That was about it."

"Kellie didn't say that the police were trying to pin the death on her?"

There was a sudden blast of rock music in the background, and Janey Mahler excused herself, then hollered, "Ashley, turn that stereo down!"

The music faded, and she was back on the line, her voice modified once again. "Oh, yes, you're right. Kellie did say that the police were doing their best to make her look guilty. And Wesley told her not to worry. 'No one is on to us,' is what he told her."

"Are you sure?"

"Positive. In those words. 'No one is on to us.' They're guilty, Mr. Mayor! I know they are."

"Have you told anyone beside Tetty and Sebastian what you overheard, Ms. Mahler?"

"No. And I don't want to. If those two find out I know what they were up to . . . well, I'm afraid of them, Mr. Mayor," she added nervously. "I live here alone with my daughter, and I couldn't sleep last night just thinking about this whole thing. Please don't tell anyone what I've told you. Not even the police."

"I won't, Ms. Mahler," I assured her. "Don't worry. You'll be fine."

I hung up and allowed myself a moment to muse over what she had said. It certainly looked as though Kellie Farrell and Wesley Fisk were up to something. But as a former lawyer, and as a savvy politician, I know better than anyone that things aren't always as they seem.

I dialed the number Nolan MacDougall had left for me, which had a 201 New Jersey area code. That probably meant it was his new house in Saddle River.

I was disappointed when an answering machine picked up, and Nolan MacDougall's recorded voice informed me that he wasn't available to take my call. I figured he was probably at the Regal Theater and contemplated running over to catch him there after the show. But to tell you the truth, I was exhausted. I didn't want to go anywhere except to bed.

After leaving a message, I replaced the phone in the cradle and wandered off to the kitchen. My stomach was rumbling and I realized I hadn't eaten in hours. Of course my chef, Lucien, was long-gone. But in the refrigerator, I found the makings for a roast beef on pumpernickel with Dijon mustard and a crisp green salad with peppercorn Parmesan dressing and a sprinkling of crumbly white feta cheese.

There was pie, too—Lucien's delectable French Silk masterpiece. I started to take a huge slice; then, remembering doctor's orders, cut it in two and deposited the slightly larger half on my plate. I supposed I should speak with Lucien about not tempting me with his rich desserts. Maybe he could devise a low-fat French Silk recipe.

Knowing Lucien, a true connoisseur, he'd roll his eyes at the offensive suggestion and toss me out of 'his' kitchen.

I ate in front of the television in my room, losing myself in an old episode of a seventies detective series. The clues were blatant and the murderer obvious from the start.

Could things be that simple in real life, though?

Somehow, I had the feeling that, while Kellie Farrell and Wesley Fisk were obvious suspects, the Matthews case wasn't as cut and dried as it seemed.

Still, my lunch with Ms. Farrell tomorrow promised to be interesting, to say the least.

SEVEN

Before my lunch with Kellie, I spent some time Wednesday evening reading everything I could get my hands on—thanks to Sybil and my old stash of *Playbills*—about her, Conor Matthews, and *The Last Laugh*.

Her bio was fairly standard. She'd grown up in Indiana and gone to college at Northwestern. In addition to her television commercials and her work on the soap *The Midnight Hour*, she'd had roles with touring company productions of *Carousel* and *Oklahoma*. Of course. She had that all-American apple pie look that was perfect for Rodgers and Hammerstein.

Her Broadway debut had been as a chorus member in *Les Misérables*. She'd had a small role in *Beauty and the Beast*, and one in an obscure play that had opened and closed in the same week. The role of Amber Blue was her first lead.

Conor Matthews, as I already knew, had done bit parts in small-time Shakespearean productions before training with the Royal Shakespeare Company in London a few years back.

Though he'd long coveted a position in that respected conservatory and won it only after repeated auditions, he'd returned to the states to play Romeo in a Broadway revival of *Romeo and Juliet* last year.

It was a perfectly dreadful take on the Bard's romantic tragedy, as I recall. Rather than using Shakespeare's warring families and the seventeenth-century Verona setting, that particular production had taken place in Philadelphia in the year 2000. They'd made Juliet into an aspiring rap singer, and Romeo was an alien.

Needless to say, the show had closed promptly, after hideous reviews.

Conor Matthews, in his interview with Sybil, had been reluctant to discuss the *Romeo and Juliet* debacle, and understandably so. But reading between the lines, I discerned that the experience had left him more of a classical theater snob than ever. And I definitely sensed that he was restless, perhaps even chagrined over his role in a splashy production like *The Last Laugh*. He wasn't doing what he wanted to do with his career, that much was clear.

It was beginning to show, I think, in his performances as Quincy Tate. I read a series of recent reviews, most of which pointed out that, while he was competent in the role and his voice was wonderful, he seemed to lack the passion Beau Walton had brought to the show. One critic even came right out and mentioned that Nolan MacDougall was considering bringing Walton back in . . . "And well he should. Conor Matthews doesn't belong in *The Last Laugh* any more than aliens and rap singers belonged in *Romeo and Juliet.*"

I hoped that Kellie Farrell could shed some light on Conor Matthews's state of mind these last few months—and on her own role in his life . . . and, perhaps, in his death.

Walking into Le Cirque at the height of Thursday afternoon's lunch hour was like walking into a private party held exclusively for the crème de la crème of Manhattan.

There were foreign dignitaries and local moguls; bankers and philanthropists; surgeons and starlets. Every socialite in town was accounted for, each one resplendent in an understated designer ensemble and fresh-from-the-salon coif. I was faced with the usual round of encounters with friends and casual acquaintances as I made my way to the table where Kellie Farrell waited.

As luck would have it, Sybil's gossipy pal Adriana Leek and her cronies were seated at the table directly across from where Kellie Farrell sat waiting for me. Noting the way the ladies were eyeing her as I approached, I realized they had not only recognized her, but were bubbling over with curiosity, wondering what she was doing *here* and who she was meeting.

For her part, Kellie appeared, even from a distance, to have mastered the art of cool detachment necessary under such circumstances. Her blond hair was swept smoothly into an elegant chignon, and she wore something classic, tailored, and black—with a single strand of pearls.

She greeted me politely and respectfully, and if she was aware of the many sets of probing eyes on us, she didn't glance in their direction. Still, something told me she was fully aware of the attention; that it didn't bother her in the least.

Our table was as private as possible and my bodyguards scattered and made themselves discreet, yet I knew nothing we did would escape the interested parties surrounding us. At least they wouldn't be able to hear what we said, if we kept our voices low, as I had every intention of doing.

"How have you been these past few days?" I asked Kellie as we settled in with drinks—chardonnay for her, a Tanqueray and tonic for me.

She shrugged. "Not good. Not only do I have to mourn my loss, but I have to worry about being thrown in jail for something I didn't do."

I raised an eyebrow at her bluntness. "What makes you think you're going to be arrested?"

"Just a feeling," she said, twirling the stem of her wineglass between her manicured fingers. "I know they're thinking I did it."

"Who is thinking that?"

"The police. Everyone else."

"Did you?" I asked abruptly, looking her in the eye.

She met my gaze without flinching. "Absolutely not. No. I did not."

"Then you have nothing to worry about," I said, as if I believed that—and her.

She laughed bitterly. "You're a lawyer, Mr. Mayor. You know better than anyone that the guilty often go free—and the innocent are occasionally punished."

"Who, in your opinion, is the guilty party in this case?"

I caught her gaze darting around the room, as though to gauge the audience. She was an actress to the core, performing even now. "I wish I knew," she said, shaking her head sadly—and a bit dramatically, in my opinion. "Why anyone would want poor Conor dead is beyond me."

"Could it have been an accident?" I inquired, knowing full well that it wasn't.

"Are you kidding? Real bullets do not march themselves into guns. And real bullets would have no business being among the props for our show. No one would take a chance like that, knowing that a mixup could occur."

I knew as much, having read the published interviews with the production propertyman and stage manager. In fact, they were on my mental list of people to question, once I'd heard what Kellie had to say.

"Mr. Mayor," she said earnestly, "someone brought those real bullets to the theater, and someone put them into the gun. Someone who wanted my fiancé dead. It's that simple."

I nodded. "But who? You must have some idea. Did Conor have any enemies?"

"Not *enemies* . . ."

"All right," I said, rephrasing my question, "Who, in your opinion, wasn't as crazy about Conor as you were?"

"There were a few people, I suppose," she said. She sighed melodramatically. Her every word, every gesture continued to seem deliberate, as she played to the audience of diners. "See, Conor had . . . well, he kind of had an attitude. But a lot of actors do."

"What do you mean?"

"He was classically trained. He thrived on what he thought of as *real* theater."

"Tennessee Williams and Thornton Wilder?" I asked, as though I didn't know where she was leading.

"No. Shakespeare, Mr. Mayor. He'd trained at the Royal Shakespeare Company in London. He wanted to become a great Shakespearean actor. That was his true ambition in life. To become known for playing characters like King Lear and Othello."

"I read that just before landing the Quincy Tate role, he starred in a production of *Romeo and Juliet.*"

She rolled her eyes. "Yeah. That lasted about a minute. It was horrible. Conor told me he was devastated when it ended, though. Luckily, he was looking for work just when Nolan MacDougall was recasting Quincy Tate. Actually, he might not have said 'luckily.' "

"Did he think *The Last Laugh* was beneath him?"

She tilted her head, sipped her wine thoughtfully. "Not *beneath* him. Just . . . not what he wanted to be doing. For a long time, Shakespeare wasn't exactly what mainstream audiences wanted to see on Broadway. They wanted razzle-dazzle entertainment, big production numbers. They wanted helicopters landing on stage, falling chandeliers. They wanted real vintage cars," she added, referring, of course, to the big production number in *The Last Laugh*.

"But that's changed?"

"It hasn't changed; they still want that, but tastes seem to be broadening lately. There have been some phenomenally successful Shakespearean productions. Like the recent revival of *The Tempest.*"

I nodded. "And it bothered Conor that he wasn't a part of that scene."

"In a way. But he was no fool. He wasn't about to turn down the chance to star in a big show. I think he planned to use it as a stepping-stone to what he really wanted. First, he'd get the wealth, the fame—"

"Those things were really important to him?"

"Aren't they important to every actor?"

"Including yourself, Miss Farrell?" I neatly responded to her question with one of my own.

She regarded me coolly. "Of course—to an extent. I do what I do because of my love of the art, Mr. Mayor. But would I mind having five homes and a chauffeur, and being adored by millions of fans? Not a bit."

"Don't overestimate fame," I advised her dryly, sipping my gin and glancing toward my bodyguards scattered around the dining room. "It can be a bit of a hindrance."

"Being obscure is worse—particularly for an actor," she pointed out, as our meals arrived.

"Getting back to Conor," I said, after tasting my grilled rosemary lamb and finding it savory and succulent, just as I'd anticipated, "Who were his enemies? Give me names."

"I told you he didn't have enemies."

"All right," I said with exaggerated patience, "who wouldn't rush to be first in line to become president of the Conor Matthews fan club?"

"Well . . . I suppose Beau Walton wouldn't."

"Because he was jealous that Conor had stepped into his role?"

"Maybe. I don't really know the man; I'm just speculating."

"I see. How about Wesley Fisk?"

She didn't choke on her raddichio or spill her wine. Nothing that blatant. Yet I knew, looking into her ice-blue eyes, that I'd rattled her.

"What makes you say that?" she asked, after just enough hesitation to confirm every rumor that she'd been sleeping with Fisk behind Matthews's back.

"I'm going to be perfectly honest with you, Ms. Farrell. I know that you and Wesley Fisk are having an affair."

This time, her eyes widened perceptibly and she actually did set down her fork.

For a long moment, she said nothing. And for the first time, I sensed that she'd forgotten the well-heeled crowd whose glances still shifted occasionally in our direction. She genuinely seemed flustered, caught up in a quandary over how to respond to my accusation.

"All right," she said at last. "I won't lie to you. You're absolutely correct about Wesley and me. I've been in love with him for a while now."

I nodded, satisfied that the expression on her beautiful face was one of integrity.

"But," she added, her voice turning frosty as a strawberry shake at Serendipity, "the fact that I was two-timing Conor doesn't mean that I wanted him dead—or that I killed him."

I stared at her. She stared right back at me.

"What about a conversation you and Wesley had in the parking lot of the funeral home on Monday night?"

Panic was evident in her eyes. "What are you talking about?"

"You were overheard," I informed her, "talking about the murder with Wesley. I believe he told you not to worry and said, 'No one is on to us'?"

She was silent, and then, when she spoke, fury made her words clipped and low. "Do you have me bugged, Mr. Mayor? Or do you have spies trailing my every move?"

"Neither." I speared a glazed baby carrot and popped it into my mouth. "But you were speaking in a public place, Ms. Farrell, and someone happened to overhear you. I just wondered if you'd care to explain."

"Yes, I would care to explain, as a matter of fact. What Wesley meant was that no one was on to our affair. He and I are both fully aware that it wouldn't look good for either of us if the world found out we were seeing each other behind Conor's back."

"I see."

"I'm telling you the truth, Mr. Mayor," she said levelly.

And I decided, in that instant, that she was. You may think I'm a fool, that I let a pretty face and some smooth talk sway me into believing rubbish.

Think whatever you want. You weren't sitting at that table in Le Cirque, looking her in the eye. I was, and I'm telling you that Kellie Farrell was not guilty of murdering Conor Matthews. I believed her story.

I told her as much, which caused her to break into a relieved smile and pick up her fork again.

"But," I said in an I-mean-business tone, "I'm not so sure about Wesley Fisk."

She flared up instantly. "He didn't kill Conor!"

"How do you know?"

"Because Wesley wouldn't do something like that! *Why* would he do something like that?"

I stated the obvious. "To get his romantic rival out of the picture?"

"That's ridiculous. Wesley knew he had nothing to worry about," she said, then clamped her mouth shut resolutely. She toyed moodily with a slivered almond on her plate.

"Oh? But you were engaged to Conor," I reminded her. "In fact, your engagement was announced in the *Times* just over a week ago, wasn't it?"

"Yes, but I was planning to break it off. I knew what I was doing wasn't fair to any of us—Conor, or Wesley, or me."

"Why did you wait so long to call off the engagement? You and Wesley, according to my sources"—Sybil, of course—"have been an item for several weeks now."

"Because," she said, hesitated, and continued, "you don't know Conor. He was very . . ."

"Very what?"

"He had a temper. He was unpredictable. And I was afraid of what he'd do when I told him that I couldn't marry him."

"You mean he was violent?"

"No. Not that I've ever seen, but . . . it's nothing specific, Mr. Mayor. I just always had the impression that Conor had a dark side. That he appeared to be a calm, almost passive personality, but that if I ever crossed him . . ."

"He'd explode and harm you?"

"Maybe not *me* . . ."

"Wesley?"

"I don't know. But I will tell you something that I never mentioned to the police," she said, leaning across the table as if to alert me that she was about to reveal a bombshell.

I followed suit.

"I'm positive I smelled liquor on Conor's breath during that last performance." Her voice was a mere whisper.

I raised my eyebrows. "I thought he didn't drink."

"Nothing stronger than Mountain Dew," she confirmed. "He always had several cans of it in his dressing room during a performance. I think the caffeine wired him for the stage, or something. But on Saturday night, I swear he'd been drinking booze. I smelled it on his breath in every scene we had together."

"Why, in your opinion, would he have been drinking?"

"He wouldn't have, under any circumstances. That's why I think someone must have slipped the booze into his Mountain Dew."

I pondered that. "Why would anyone do that?"

"I have no idea."

I frowned. It certainly didn't make sense.

"If you can imagine Conor ever falling off the wagon," I pressed Kellie, "what would be the cause?"

"I told you, I can't—"

"I know what you told me. But on the off chance that Conor was responsible for feeding himself the liquor—if he actually was drinking of his own free will, and not because someone had spiked his Mountain Dew—what would have caused him to do it?"

"I guess . . ." She looked dubious. "I guess if he were extremely nervous or upset about something. Maybe if he'd had an encounter of some sort with someone who didn't like him. But, Mr. Mayor, I really can't imagine someone like Conor taking it upon himself to drink liquor under any circumstances."

"Why," I asked her, "didn't you tell the police about this?"

"Why should I?" She lifted her chin stubbornly. "After the way they've treated me, I'm not going to offer anything they don't ask about directly. Besides, they'd assume that Conor was distraught over something I'd done, and they'd use that as evidence against me."

"I see. And why did you tell me?"

"Because you're different, Mr. Mayor. I trust you."

"Good. And thank you for sharing that observation."

I filed away the revelation about the booze, intrigued.

Then I commented, "I assume Wesley Fisk is a man of infinite patience."

She blinked. "What do you mean?"

"He wasn't putting pressure on you to break it off with Conor? He told you to take all the time you needed, that he'd be there, waiting for you?" I swallowed another delicious morsel of lamb.

"Not exactly," she admitted. "He was getting frustrated. Anyone would," she added defensively. "But he understood that I needed to do things my way."

"Ms. Farrell," I said, "is it possible that Conor found out about you and Wesley, and that he may have threatened Wesley, and that Wesley in turn—"

"No!" she interrupted. "There's no way Conor knew about us."

"No way?" I was actually amused, and pointed out, "*I* knew. What makes you think he didn't?"

She frowned slightly. "How did you find out?"

"Gossip," I said truthfully, though not about to name my sources. "It was all over town, to tell you the truth."

"All right," she said quietly after a moment's reflection. "Maybe Conor could conceivably have suspected that something was going on between me and Wesley. But he never confronted Wesley."

"How do you know?"

"Wesley would have told me," she said promptly.

"So you trust him?"

"Of course I trust him," she snapped.

"I see. So you're telling me that if Wesley had replaced the blanks with real bullets in order to remove a very real obstacle from the path to living happily ever after with you, you would have been aware of it."

"Yes, I would have been aware," she said, "and I certainly would have talked him out of it if I'd known . . . *not* that Wesley is capable of doing something like that."

I would be the judge of that, I decided.

"Then you won't mind if I take his phone number and discuss this with him," I told her, and pulled a pen and pad from my briefcase, which was tucked beneath the table.

"*I* won't mind," she said tersely, "but I can't speak for him. He's as fed up as I am with questions and suspicions."

"If he's as innocent as you are, he'll be just as eager to clear his name, Ms. Farrell."

She considered that, then nodded, and reluctantly gave me the number.

I wondered why she'd agreed to talk to me—rather, suggested it herself!—in the first place.

I got my answer as we left the restaurant. Ms. Kellie Farrell swept out of the room with the grace and stage presence of a diva at the Met. She knew just as well as I did that every gossip column in town—with the exception, of course, of Sybil's—would have an item about our lunch together.

It had never hurt an up-and-coming actress to be seen lunching at Le Cirque with one of the most well-known, well-liked men in New York City.

Ms. Farrell's agenda was just as I'd suspected. Fame and fortune. Nothing more.

And thus, Suspect Number One was effectively and officially knocked off my list.

Nolan MacDougall tracked me down with a phone call just as I was leaving City Hall that evening.

"Mr. Mayor," he said, sounding positively jovial, "I've been wanting to talk to you."

"So I gathered. I got your message."

"And I got yours, but not until just now. I stayed in my pied-à-terre last night after the show. I was too exhausted to drive all the way back to Jersey."

"That is exhausting," I agreed wryly. Saddle River is a hop, skip, and jump from the George Washington Bridge at that hour of the evening.

"How's the show going?" I asked him.

"Wonderfully! Sold out from now until doomsday!" he exclaimed, a little too effusively. He immediately moderated his voice and added, "Of course, it sickens me that it took someone's brutal murder to turn the box office around."

"It sickens me, too," I replied. *And so do you.* "What can I do for you, Nolan?"

"I know you're investigating the Conor Matthews murder, and I thought we could discuss it."

"I see." I rubbed my chin. "Do you have some inside information for me?"

"No," he said, sounding taken aback. "But I thought you might have some for me."

I put him on the spot, and must admit I enjoyed the image of him squirming in his Stickley chair on the other end of the line. "What do you mean by that, Nolan?"

"I just wondered . . . I've cooperated with the police, told them what I know—which, incidentally, is nothing—but they won't tell me anything about the investigation. You and I are old friends—"

Friends, I thought, was pushing it, given the fact that I can't stand the man and he reportedly can't stand me.

"—and I figured," he went on, "that you'd fill me in."

"What did you want to know?"

He hesitated. "Well, obviously, I was wondering who killed Matthews, according to the NYPD."

"If they knew, they'd be making an arrest," I pointed out.

"I suppose, but . . . Well, do you know who they suspect?"

So that was it. He sounded nervous enough for me to promptly transfer his name into bold italics with a double underline on my own suspect list. "I have no idea," I told him. "Who do you suspect, Nolan?"

"I—I have no idea, either," he told me. "Say, how's that little school chancellor problem coming along? I read in this morning's paper that . . ."

As he rattled on in a jittery voice about nothing that made any sense, I asked myself whether he was curious about the case—which, after all, involved the death of his leading man—for professional reasons . . . or personal reasons.

"We should get together for dinner sometime soon, Nolan," I commented just before we hung up. I knew I'd want to question him, but I wasn't ready for that just yet. Still, I knew it would have to be soon—and next week wasn't looking very flexible, thanks to several business trips on my agenda.

"Er—yes, we should. Let's do that," he agreed vaguely.

And that was that.

I wasn't surprised to see that my lunch with Kellie Farrell was mentioned in two different tabloid gossip columns on Friday.

One columnist observed that "the bachelor mayor and the newly available Ms. Farrell gazed nonstop into each other's eyes, seemingly oblivious that anyone else was in the room."

The other—the ever lurid Clancy O'Brien—described Kellie Farrell as "heartbreakingly dignified in her somber black mourning garb," and me as "gentle and sympathetic, gallantly protecting her from the probing eyes of the crowd."

Both columns speculated on my romantic involvement with Conor Matthews's fiancée, mentioning that I was, of course, investigating the case and seemed to have fallen for her in the process.

Naturally, my parents got wind of this and saw fit to call City Hall on Friday afternoon from somewhere in the Caribbean.

"Eddie," Mom trilled over faint steel drum music in the background, "are you in love?"

"No, Ma," I said, shaking my head in disgust. "Where are you?"

"At sea," she said vaguely. "Wait, your father's grabbing the phone."

"Eddie?" Bernard Koch's voice boomed across hundreds of miles, causing me to wince and hold the phone slightly away from my ear. "What's going on? You got yourself a new girlfriend?"

I sighed. "No, Pop. I had a business lunch with someone, and you know what the tabloids are capable of doing. How the heck did you find out way down there?"

"Your mother called your sister in Scarsdale this morning to remind her to tape Regis and Kathy Lee—Engelbert Humperdinck was going to be on. Anyway, Sophie told her what the morning papers said."

"I didn't know Sophie read the tabloids."

"She doesn't. Melissa"—that would be Sophie's daughter and my niece, who lives on the Upper West Side with her husband and newborn son—"called her and told her that she heard at her Mommy and Me class that you were getting married."

"What?"

"Sophie was very upset that she was the last to know. You know how she hates when people keep secrets from her," Pop said. "And as soon as your mother heard, she went to see the cruise director about arranging for a helicopter to pick us up from the ship and fly us back to the mainland."

"Pop," I began, then squeezed my eyes shut and shook my head, not even sure where to start. How I managed to remain calm, I'll never know.

"Listen to me very carefully," I said succinctly. "I am not—repeat, *not*—getting married. So Sophie doesn't have to worry about being left out of the plans. And you and Ma do not have to be airlifted from the boat. All I did was have a business lunch with someone."

"Anyone I know?"

My father, who lived in metropolitan New York City for over

seventy years, often seems to operate under the illusion that it's like a small midwestern town where no one's a stranger.

"No, Pop," I said patiently. "You don't know her. She's an actress."

"So I hear. You know I've always liked people in show biz. I've always said they're not afraid to show their emotions."

"Mmm hmm."

"And you're trying to solve the case of this actress's boyfriend's murder, is that right?"

"That's right." I should have known better than to think there's anyplace in the world where my business isn't public knowledge.

"That's what I hear. What'd you find out so far, Eddie?"

"Not much," I admitted. "But I'm working on it."

"Do you want me to come back early? I can give you a hand like I did on the Krieg case last—"

"No!" I blurted. "No, Pop, you enjoy your cruise. You deserve it."

"What, I deserve to bake and sweat in a deck chair all day and sleep in a bed that rocks back and forth like a hammock? And you know I've never liked hammocks. I'll tell you, Eddie, this cruise is no picnic. I can't even find anyone who knows how to play pinochle."

"How about shuffleboard?"

"I should stand around in the hot sun and poke little flat things with a stick all day long?"

"Well, what about the food, Pop?"

"What about it? These cruise people don't know from food. You can't even get a decent bagel in the morning, and every time I order a seltzer, it's flat. Yes, it is, Lil," he argued with my mother, who could be heard disputing him in the background.

"Listen, Pop, this call is costing you a fortune—"

"It is? How do you know that?"

"Ship to shore can't be cheap," I pointed out.

That got him off the line in a hurry, with a promise to call me as soon as they got to New York two weeks from Saturday. Thank God, they were staying with my uncle Mort, Pop's brother, on Long Island.

I reminded them that I'd be out of town when they got here—

I had a meeting in Washington Friday and a conference in Texas over the weekend.

"Washington?" Pop asked hurriedly, ever mindful of the rising toll. "If you bump into your pal the President, see if you can find out what's going on with your mother's social security check. It's been—"

"Pop, I doubt I'll be seeing the President, and even if I did, he's too busy to look into Mom's check."

"Eddie, what did I always tell you growing up? If you need an answer, go straight to the top. See what you can do."

Did I say, earlier, that I missed my parents?

I take it back, every word of it. They mean well, and I love them dearly, but I have never been so glad to have them far, far away.

_____EIGHT

Like most Manhattanites, I like to escape on the weekends. But while many city dwellers trade their urban apartments for country cottages or beach houses, I trade my high-gloss Upper East Side mansion for my cozy apartment on Washington Place in the Village. That way, I don't have to leave the city I love in order to obtain a much-needed change of scenery and some peace of mind. All I have to do is hop on the subway and head downtown.

I've heard there are people who don't believe I actually ride the public transportation in New York—people who assume I take my chauffeur-driven limo everywhere I go.

The truth is, there's no better way for a mayor to comprehend the perks and problems of his city than to experience the lifestyle alongside its citizens. That's why you're just as likely to find me sitting next to you on the Downtown Number Two Express train as you are to find a weary secretary heading home to Brooklyn or a security guard heading to his night shift at the World Trade Center.

I'm happy to report that while I generally sleep well at Gracie Mansion—barring my hiatus hernia which lets the stomach acids back into my throat, or some city disaster—I tend to get the soundest sleep of all when I spend the night at my apartment.

I have a wonderful old brass bed that I bought for nine dollars at a farm auction years ago, and it's the most comfortable bed in the world. Granted, Gracie Mansion is no cold-water flat, but I can always relax best here in the Village, surrounded by my familiar belongings and the night sounds of Washington Place.

On this particular Saturday morning, rather than puttering around my apartment as I'm usually apt to do, I was up and dressed by seven-thirty. I had decided to devote most of my day to the Matthews case, though I did have some official business to handle in between. Still, my schedule was fairly free of mayoral commitments, and those I had were relatively lightweight: a ribbon-cutting ceremony at a new apartment tower in Chelsea and a benefit auction later this afternoon on Madison Avenue.

After a quick breakfast of grapefruit juice and, of course, two strong cups of Martinson's coffee—it always tastes best brewed in the Chemex I've had for years—I scanned the list of appointments I'd made for myself for the day.

First on the list was a visit to the medical examiner's office, which is on the East Side, near Bellevue. I wanted to ask some questions about the autopsy that had been done on Conor Matthews. Normally, the authorities might bristle at an outsider snooping around official autopsy records, but when you're mayor, you can expect them to be slightly more accommodating.

Besides, Darius Jones, a forensic pathologist who works at the coroner's office, owed me a big favor. Once, at a catered Christmas party at the Rainbow Room, he happened to mention to me that he adored the special green peppercorn pâté on the hors d'oeuvre buffet, but had no idea where one would find it.

The next morning, I sent him a whole one—the size of a babka from Zabar's—straight from a wholesaler friend of mine on Greenwich Street. Darius, ever grateful, had told me to give him a call if I ever needed anything.

So I had, yesterday, and he'd agreed to meet with me at nine in his office.

I took the subway across town and uptown. The trains were running like clockwork and I only had to wait thirty seconds to switch at Union Square, so I got there twenty minutes early. Darius happened to be in and available. Wonderful. The day was starting smoothly, which I took as a good omen.

Once we were seated in the privacy of his office, Darius settled back in his chair. "Tell me what this is about, Mr. Mayor. I know you're looking into Conor Matthews's death—"

"The whole city knows that."

"Well, you're the mayor. People are interested in what you're doing."

I shrugged and continued, "I want to see your autopsy report on Matthews."

He looked as though he'd known that was coming, and pursed his lips briefly before saying, "I was afraid of that. With all due respect, you know that information is available only to family members and lawyers—"

"I'm a lawyer," I pointed out.

"You know what I mean . . . You— You're not representing Matthews."

"Not technically, but—"

"And anyway," he interjected, "why do you need to look at the file? We released the pertinent information. Matthews died of a gunshot wound. Besides, there were hundreds of witnesses to his death. Weren't you one of them?"

"Yes, I was. But I'm interested in the toxicological evidence. You did do a full medical-legal autopsy on him, didn't you?"

"Of course. Since the death was ruled a homicide, we were required to."

"So you did draw and test his blood."

"Yes, but the results aren't back from the lab yet."

"When will they be back?"

He shrugged. "Weeks . . . could be months. In Matthews's case, the cause of death has already been ruled, so the toxicology tests are basically superfluous."

Disappointed, I pondered that for a moment, then asked, "Would you mind getting the file, Darius?"

"I don't see why—"

"It's been a while since you've tasted that peppercorn pâté, isn't it, Darius? Bet you'd love some. And I could arrange for you to have it, if you'll just help me out here."

The man was amazing. He broke down more quickly than a reluctant dieter in a pastry shop. He shrugged and said, "Be right back."

While he was gone, I studied the family photo on his desk. He had a pretty, young wife who was the spitting image of Natalie Cole and three adorable children. I wondered what it was like for a family man like Jones to be immersed in death and tragedy every day, as he was. Not easy, that was for sure.

I was having a hard enough time, myself, dealing with a murder on a daily basis. Conor Matthews's death was never far from my mind. I kept remembering his crumpled body on the stage, kept thinking of how his life had drained away on that river of blood before anyone watching realized what was happening. No one should have to leave this world in such a grisly manner.

When Darius returned, he sat down, opened the file, and scanned several pages.

"Well?" I prodded, tapping my pen against the edge of his desk impatiently. "Can I see the file?"

"Just as I said, Mr. Mayor . . . there's nothing out of the ordinary here." He looked up. "Matthews died from a bullet wound to the heart. Case closed."

"What kind of bullet was used?" I asked.

He sighed and glanced down at the report again. "The soft-point variety. Those are metal-cased bullets with a lead tip that mushrooms on impact, increasing the striking energy. Whoever selected those deadly things wanted to be sure the job was done efficiently."

I nodded grimly. "Anything else of interest there?"

He rattled off some technical information that shed no further light on the case.

I thanked him, promised to have the pâté on his desk by Monday afternoon, and asked him to please notify me when the toxicology tests came back.

Then I headed out into the crisp September sunshine. It really was my lucky day, as I suspected earlier—a cab was just pulling up at the curb to deposit a passenger. I hopped in and gave the address of my next appointment: the Regal Theater on West Forty-sixth Street.

I don't know what I was expecting the propertyman of *The Last Laugh* to look like, but Dan Marinowski, who was waiting as promised by the stage door, was hardly what I'd ever have imagined. He was in his midthirties or so; burly and bearded, and the gray Guns N' Roses T-shirt stretched over his potbelly was stained with something that looked like spaghetti sauce. The scent of marijuana clung to him, and his eyes looked suspiciously bright.

He greeted me with a gruff "Pleased to meet ya, Mr. Mayor," and flashed a wide grin that revealed a rotting, dark gray tooth.

"Likewise. Thank you for agreeing to speak with me, Mr. Marinowski."

"It's Dan. No problem." He stubbed out his cigarette—the legal kind, though I had no doubt he'd recently been smoking something else—against the concrete wall of the theater. Then he opened the door, which was propped open with a broom, and motioned for me to step inside.

"Security guard doesn't get here till noon," he commented. "Had to leave the door open."

"How did you get into the theater?" I asked.

"Made arrangements with Stan, the house manager. He works for the Regal," he told me. "He's always here. He let me in. There are a few other people around because of the matinee later, but the place is pretty much empty in the mornings."

"I see."

"The cops have been all over this place ever since last week," Dan informed me, leading me through a musty hallway.

"I'm sure they have."

"They showed up yesterday morning and wanted to search the whole place. Private dressing rooms and everything. But management wouldn't let them without a warrant."

"Is that so?" I knew that sooner or later, they'd be back with a warrant.

Though we didn't encounter anyone on our journey, I heard voices here and there—a man having an animated telephone conversation from behind the closed door of an office; the muffled sounds of two females laughingly discussing something.

"I've probably talked to half a dozen different detectives and reporters," Dan went on as our footsteps echoed in the deserted hallway. "Told 'em all the same thing. I have no idea who switched those blanks for bullets, but it sure as hell wasn't me."

"Of course not." I hadn't labeled Dan a suspect before meeting him, and now I wasn't inclined to. Everything about him was straightforward and relaxed. I wondered whether the police were considering him a suspect. He certainly didn't seem worried, if they were.

"What did you think of Conor Matthews?" I asked casually as we turned a corner and headed down another long corridor.

Dan shrugged. "Didn't really know him. He kept his distance from the techies. But I guess he was an all-right guy—except he sure as hell wasn't much fun."

"What do you mean?"

"He had a thing about drinking. Got all put out if someone only had one beer, even. I heard him telling Lara Marie once, that she was the only person in the cast, besides him, who was smart enough to avoid booze."

"Lara Marie . . . ?" The name sounded vaguely familiar.

"Landry. She plays Trixie DeLong."

Oh, right. Lara Marie Landry. She'd been superb as the cheap showgirl with a heart of gold and a crush on Quincy Tate.

"Were Conor and Lara Marie friends, then?" I asked, intrigued.

Another shrug. "Guess so. Here we are."

He opened a door and we stepped into what appeared to be a vast storage area filled with pieces of sets and fake lampposts, street signs, that sort of thing.

He led me through the surreal maze to a cabinet on wheels.

"In here," he said, thumping it, "I keep the props for Act Two."

"Is it kept locked?"

He hesitated slightly before saying, "Yep."

"Can you open it for me?"

"Sure." He patted the back pockets of his jeans, then fumbled inside. "Be right back," he said after a moment, looking a bit abashed. "I must'a left my keys with my stuff upstairs in the green room."

I nodded. While he was gone, I wandered around the storage area, noting that there were lots of places where an intruder could hide, watching the cabinet, and waiting for a chance to tamper with the gun.

"Here we go," Dan said, showing up again and waving a jangling key ring. He fiddled with the lock on the cabinet for a moment, trying different keys, then popped the door open.

There, sitting quietly on the shelf, was the gun that had killed Conor Matthews.

"This isn't the gun that killed Matthews," Dan said, as though he'd read my mind. "The cops took that one right away. This is a replacement."

He handed it over to me and watched as I inspected it. A Smith & Wesson Ladysmith .38 Special.

"These are blanks," Dan informed me, taking the gun back and emptying several cartridges into his palm.

I nodded.

"Where's the gun kept when it's not onstage during the final scene?" I asked as Dan Marinowski replaced the cartridges, one by one, into the rotating cylinder.

"Right in here," he said, gesturing at the cabinet. "All the props for the second act are here, like I said."

I glanced over the contents.

Among other things, there were vaudeville hats and canes for Hugo and Quincy's dance routine, Trixie DeLong's ornate silver powder compact, and a stack of folded pale blue handkerchiefs, identical to the one Amber uses to wipe Quincy's fake blood from her hands after he's shot.

"I notice that the cabinet is on wheels. Is it always kept in this storage room?"

"Nope. It's rolled into the wings right before the performance."

"Who has access to this cabinet?"

Dan shrugged. "I do. And Teresa. She's the stage manager."

I already knew that, having attempted to make an appointment with her. Her assistant had informed me that Ms. Jaffe would get back to me, but she hadn't, so far.

"So you each have a key," I told Dan. "You and Teresa."

"Right."

"And no one else does."

"Like I told that detective, Charley Beacon—"

"Deacon."

"Yeah. I told him that as far as I know, me and Teresa are the only ones who can get into the cabinet. I know *I* didn't have anything to do with Matthews's death. And if you knew Teresa, you'd know she was innocent, too. She's not the murdering type."

I fought the urge to smile at that comment, wondering what, exactly, he considered the murdering type to be.

I asked, "Where do you keep your keys, Mr. Marinowski?"

"In my pocket. Usually," he tacked on a bit sheepishly.

"But there are times when you lose track of them?"

"Not usually. Just once in a while."

"Earlier, when I asked you about the cabinet being locked, you seemed to hesitate."

"I did?"

"You did."

"Oh." He contemplated that, then said reluctantly, "See, a few months ago, I accidentally locked my keys inside my car when I parked it in the garage on Forty-seventh. I live up in Rockland County, and I drive into the city for the performance every day. Anyway, Teresa was sick that night so she wasn't here, and we had a hard time tracking down a spare set before the curtain went up. After that," he looked around and lowered his voice to a whisper, "I've been leaving the cabinet open most of the time."

I nodded. "And who knew that?"

"I don't think anyone did. Teresa would have a cow if she knew I wasn't locking up the props. See, things tend to disappear from sets—especially cool props. Like, when I worked on *Fiddler,* everyone wanted to walk off with the red vodka glasses they used in the drinking scene. I had to guard them with my life."

"But you didn't guard these props with your life," I pointed out.

He looked uncomfortable. "Well, see, I almost got fired after that thing with the keys, so I wanted to make sure it didn't happen again. That's why I don't always lock the cabinet. Because I'd be in big trouble if I couldn't get into it again."

"And how about the theater? Is it locked?"

"The stage door? Always."

"Who has the keys?"

"Stan—the house manager. And like I said, there's a security guard there most of the time. If one of us shows up during the day, we knock and someone lets us in. Or we go around to the front.

The lobby's usually open during the day because of the ticket sales window."

"So it would be possible for someone to walk in off the street, get backstage, and replace the blanks with bullets."

He shook his head. "The theater has security," he repeated, "and most of the interior doors are kept locked. It wouldn't be easy . . ."

"But not impossible, either."

"I guess not, no." Dan put his hands into the pockets of his grungy jeans and rocked back on the heels of his black boots. "I'd really like to help you out. The cops have already asked me and everyone else just about everything you can imagine, Mr. Mayor, and they're not always the nicest guys you want to talk to."

"It's not their job to charm people." It wasn't mine, either, although I do my best, most of the time.

"I didn't tell them about not locking the cabinet," he said. "I was afraid they'd tell Teresa, and she'd fire me. I really need this job. My uncle—he's in the business, he's a wig supervisor for *Miss Saigon*—had to pull a lot of strings to get it for me. You can't say a word to anyone, okay?"

"Okay, Dan. I'll keep it to myself," I promised. "Thanks for being up front with me."

"No problem. I figured I could trust you. After all, you're the mayor."

See? I told you I could be charming. I have to admit, I really have a way of winning people over.

Most people, anyway.

Wesley Fisk wasn't one of them.

The moment he opened the door of his apartment on West Twenty-ninth Street, off Tenth Avenue, he glowered.

"Come on in," he said after I'd greeted him politely. His tone was hardly inviting, and he certainly hadn't been pleasant on the telephone when I'd called him yesterday to set up this appointment. I wondered if he was always such a grouch.

"I just want to ask you a few questions, Mr. Fisk," I said, following him into the living room.

"Good, because I'm in a hurry. Like I said, I have the matinee."

"But the performance isn't until two o'clock, correct?"

"Yeah," he muttered, plopping himself down on the nondescript blue couch.

"Then we have time for a short conversation," I pointed out.

He didn't invite me to sit, but I perched on a matching easy chair opposite him and glanced around the room. It was rectangular, with off-white walls and carpeting and a large window at one end. I speculated that it should have a view of the street twenty-six stories below, but the vertical blinds were closed.

The room was what I would call strictly functional—simple furniture, two floor lamps, and a wall unit that housed a television and stereo, as well as what appeared to be an extensive CD collection. There were no plants, no knickknacks, no photographs—no homey touches whatsoever, unless you counted two large paintings on the walls. Both were abstract art in blues and grays, not my style at all.

"Well?" Fisk was watching me, his arms folded.

I turned my attention to him. I have to admit that Wesley Fisk was a handsome man, and it wasn't hard to imagine a woman like Kellie Farrell being attracted to him. He had a handsome, chiseled face, a good build, and sandy-colored hair he wore in a style I'd noticed on many young men recently. He was dressed in a black turtleneck and baggy black slacks, an outfit that created a dramatic statement. His clothes and his attitude seemed to be saying, "Look at me . . . I'm important."

He was talented, too. His voice, I recalled from *The Last Laugh,* was a rich baritone; he was a graceful dancer and a gifted actor with remarkable stage presence.

On top of that, he had brains—and bucks. His program bio stated that he'd been educated at several formidable New England prep schools and two Ivy League universities. He'd been raised in Beverly Hills.

I'm sure the package was attractive to an ambitious woman like Kellie Farrell.

But I knew that I didn't like him. It was pure instinct, and it didn't mean that he was guilty of Conor Matthews's murder. But I sensed that this wasn't someone I'd choose to spend time with under any circumstances.

"What was your relationship with Conor Matthews?" I asked, looking him in the eye.

He bristled. "He was my costar. We worked together onstage."

"Playing romantic rivals. Your Hugo Shields to his Quincy Tate."

"Very good, Mr. Mayor. You know the show."

"I've seen it several times," I said, and complimented him on his performance, which seemed to make him relax slightly.

"Getting back to Matthews—I didn't see you at his funeral."

"No." He looked distinctly uncomfortable. "I couldn't make it."

"Why not?"

"I wasn't feeling well."

"I see." Without missing a beat, I asked, "Was Matthews aware that you were sleeping with his fiancée?"

He didn't appear surprised at my question. Kellie Farrell, I was aware, would have briefed him about what I knew.

He shook his head and said, "Not that I know of."

"You mean that he never confronted you about it."

"No, he didn't."

I studied him. He appeared outwardly calm, yet there was a palpable tension in the air. I honestly couldn't tell whether he was lying.

"Look, Mr. Mayor," he said abruptly, unfolding his arms and leaning toward me. "I know you think I bumped off Matthews to get him out of the picture with Kellie. Let me save you a lot of time and effort and tell you that I didn't."

I was silent, waiting for him to go on.

"Listen, *I'm* the one who fired the gun!" He was practically shouting, as though I'd offered an argument. He jumped up and paced across the room. "Do you think I'm stupid enough, if I were going to kill the guy, to do it in cold blood, in front of a thousand people?"

I didn't point out that, on the contrary, it would have been a clever means of disposing of the enemy, since he was merely following the script, which called for him to shoot Matthews.

"You certainly had a motive to have killed him," I observed after a moment.

He smirked and sat again. "Oh? And what was that?"

"Kellie had promised you she'd break it off with Matthews, and she hadn't done it. Maybe you were afraid she never would. Maybe you were afraid you'd lose her to him."

"I was never afraid of that. There's no contest between me and Matthews. He had a lot of hang-ups. Drove Kellie nuts. She was taking her time dumping him because . . ." He trailed off, looking unsure of himself for the first time. But only fleetingly. He quickly regained his composure and shrugged.

"What are your feelings for her?" I asked.

"Kellie? I love her. Why?"

"Just wondering." A man like Fisk didn't seem the passionate, romantic type. It was hard to imagine him getting all worked up over his emotions.

And yet, maybe he had been obsessed with possessing a woman he couldn't have.

Sybil had told me that Fisk was known for being a real go-getter. Ambitious and goal-oriented. He had landed his first Broadway role, as a chorus member in *Phantom of the Opera,* at twenty-two. From that point on, he'd worked steadily and won positive reviews.

Maybe Fisk had single-mindedly set out to win Kellie Farrell for himself . . .

Maybe that drive had led him to murder . . .

Maybe.

"Who do you think killed Conor Matthews?" I asked him.

He answered readily. "Beau Walton."

Surprised at his prompt response, I stared at him.

"It makes sense," he elaborated. "Walton was itching to get back into the cast. His career died the moment he stepped out of the Quincy Tate role. He's been buddying up to Nolan MacDougall for weeks, trying to squirm his way back in."

"You actually think Beau Walton would kill Conor Matthews in order to vacate the role?"

"I wouldn't put it past him. The guy's a real snake."

Of course, I'd already pinpointed Beau Walton as a possibility. But I didn't tell Fisk that.

"Did you notice anything out of the ordinary the night Matthews was killed?"

"I noticed a *lot* of things out of the ordinary, Mr. Mayor."

"Like what?" I asked, intrigued.

He clamped his mouth shut and shook his head.

"What don't you want to tell me, Wesley?"

"Anything that'll make you think the wrong thing," he said.

"Which is . . . ?"

"That Matthews was upset with me for some reason. He wasn't. I swear that he and I never had contact, other than strictly business and onstage interaction. We never had a confrontation over Kellie and me. Nothing."

"I believe you," I said, though I wasn't certain that I did. But I had to get him to talk. "What went on that night?"

"I haven't told the police any of this, okay? Because I knew that those jerks would jump to the wrong conclusion—"

"I understand. What did you notice?"

"For one thing, Matthews was hammered during his performance."

"Kellie mentioned to me that he might have been drinking."

"I know she did. I told her she shouldn't have said anything to you, but she said she trusted you. She said I should, too."

"She's a smart lady." I propped my elbow on my knee and my chin in my hand. "Tell me more about Matthews's behavior that night."

"He missed cues, dropped a bunch of lines, and screwed up a lot of the ones he did manage to say—if it weren't for me covering for him with ad libs, he'd have come off like a complete ass."

"Do you think it was because he was drunk?"

"Yeah, that, and he was obviously upset about something. But not—"

"I know. Not you. What do you think it could have been?"

"Who knows? But I'll tell you one thing . . ."

"What?"

"I caught him sneaking out of Kellie's dressing room one day the week before he was killed. I have no idea what he was doing in there, but he was definitely up to something."

"Did he see you?"

"No. I hid as soon as I spotted him. He went scurrying back down the hall to his own dressing room and shut the door."

"Are the dressing rooms kept locked?"

"Hardly ever. People share them, except for us three lead performers, and there's no reason to lock the doors. People pretty much respect one another's privacy."

"What about Kellie? Did you tell her what you saw?"

He hesitated. "No."

"Why not?"

"I didn't want to upset her. She was pretty shook up over this whole thing. I mean, she was going to dump the guy anyway, but I guess she didn't want to see him gunned down that way. I was kind of upset, myself."

"I can imagine," I said mildly. The man had, in effect, shot Conor Matthews to death in cold blood—though it had been an accident, *if* he really was innocent.

"Why," I went on, "didn't you tell Kellie about Conor sneaking into her dressing room as soon as it happened? I mean, before he was killed."

"Because—I don't know. I guess at the time, I figured he was just leaving her roses or a note or something. He did that once in a while." His expression told me what he thought of such a silly, sentimental gesture.

"How do you know that wasn't what he was doing?"

"I don't. And actually, I never asked Kellie whether he'd left her something that week. But the more I think about it, the more it seems like he was up to something. You know how you just get a gut instinct about certain things?"

I did. I had a gut instinct that Wesley Fisk wouldn't hesitate to lie to save his own skin.

"Listen, Mr. Mayor," he said abruptly, "I didn't tell the cops about this, because I didn't want them to be any more suspicious of Kellie than they already are. She told me you believe she's innocent, and since you know I'm innocent, too"— he paused, apparently for confirmation, and I obliged by nodding—"Well, I just thought you might be able to make something of this."

"I probably can," I told him. "Though I'm not sure what it is."

"Well, let me know what you find out. And in the meantime, I have to leave for the theater." He stood abruptly and motioned me toward the entryway.

"Thank you for speaking with me, Mr. Fisk," I said. "I may need to contact you again."

"Why?" His expression of relief was quickly replaced with suspicion again.

I shrugged. "To let you know what I find out about Matthews," I said, as though it were obvious. "I assume you'll want to be kept apprised of my investigation and any developments."

"Oh, of course. Thanks."

As he closed the door behind me, I moved his name to the top of my mental list of suspects.

I was on a roll, but unfortunately, official business had to take precedence over the murder case. I devoted the next several hours to the ribbon-cutting ceremony and the charity auction.

Sybil, clad in a vivid blue summer dress, was there with Claude, who had just returned from the Middle East. He's a conservative, buttoned-up kind of man, quite the opposite of his flamboyant wife. He was wearing a pair of tan slacks and a beige shirt—an ensemble that, with his dark blond hair and pale complexion, made him look like a shaft of wheat.

"I hear you've been busy, Mayor," he greeted me as we mingled at the reception following the auction.

"Oh?" I glanced at Sybil, who flashed her most charming smile.

"I've told him all about your sleuthing," she informed me.

I was hardly pleased with the faintly amused expression on Claude's face, nor with her choice of words; "sleuth" always makes me think of the Hardy Boys mysteries I read as a boy.

I may be an amateur when it comes to detective work, but I'm no slouch. I am, after all, a lawyer—not to mention the mayor of New York City.

"How's the case coming?" Claude inquired, sipping his champagne—which, I might add, blended perfectly with his monochromatic appearance.

"As a matter of fact, quite well."

"I hear the police are planning to make an arrest any day now."

That was certainly news to me. "According to whom?"

"Someone inside the NYPD leaked it to the press this morning," Sybil said, sensing that I was in the dark about this latest bulletin. She always likes to be the bearer of news—good or bad—and told me that the police were reportedly closing in on a suspect.

"I'll bet anything it's Beau Walton," she said blithely, plucking the cherry from her cocktail and nipping it from its stem, as Claude turned away to greet a colleague.

"What makes you say that?"

"He's the obvious choice. He wanted Matthews dead so that he could reclaim his role as Quincy Tate. Very simple."

"But what evidence is there against him?"

"Nothing has been said about new evidence in any of today's latest reports." She volleyed back at me, "What evidence have you uncovered in your snooping, Ed?"

"I'd really prefer you didn't refer to my investigation in that way, Sybil. 'Snooping' is your department, not mine."

"It is, isn't it," she said with a chuckle. "Fill me in, though, Ed. I'm dying of curiosity."

"To tell you the truth, I'm still gathering the facts, and I've just begun questioning suspects. I haven't drawn any conclusions yet."

"The case is really quite titillating, isn't it? Let's face it. There were a thousand eyewitnesses to the crime itself—but no one has come forward who witnessed the killer tampering with the gun before the shooting. And unless someone actually saw whoever it was sneaking the real bullets in, I don't see how the police can find proof of one specific person's guilt. It could have been anyone."

She had a point—I'd already arrived at the same realization. There were a number of suspects, all of whom, conceivably, had a motive, not to mention access to the murder weapon. But barring someone stepping forward and confessing, it wasn't going to be easy to narrow the field.

Unless the police had stumbled across a new piece of evidence.

"The key to the case, in my opinion," Sybil said, "is digging into the enigma that was Conor Matthews."

There are times when Sybil speaks even more melodramatically than she writes.

"Ed," she said, touching my sleeve, "you must seek, and find, the man behind the myth."

"And what makes you say that?" I asked her, though I'd been thinking the same thing, myself—though not nearly as eloquently.

"Because you need to find out who Matthews's enemies were. He was a private person, but no man is an island. There are always ways of finding out what you need to know. You must unlock the secrets of his personal life, Ed, before you can understand why someone would want to kill him—and who that person is."

"If you'll excuse me," I said, depositing my empty wineglass on a tray, "I think I'll head home now."

"Tired, Ed?"

I nodded, though I wasn't in the least.

Rather, I'd just realized that the matinee performance of *The Last Laugh* would be ending right about now. If traffic on Forty-second Street was as light as it should be at this hour of a Saturday afternoon, I had just enough time to get across town.

_____NINE

It isn't easy to conceal yourself in a crowd when you're the mayor of New York. As I waited beside the stage door of the Regal, along with a throng of impatient audience members who were clutching their *Playbills* and waiting for autographs, I found myself the center of attention.

I obliged when a group of senior citizens from Providence asked me to autograph their programs, and when middle-aged identical twin sisters asked me to pose with my arms around them.

"Hey, is that you, Ed?" called a voice that wasn't the least familiar. A total stranger—a young man who wore a flannel shirt despite the seventy-degree evening—worked his way over, flanked by two others who were dressed just like him.

"It's me," I acknowledged.

"I'm Clem," he said, shaking my hand. "This is Mike, and Mike."

Both Mikes shook my hand, then muttered amongst themselves, shuffling their feet on the concrete and hanging back.

"I just want to thank you, man," Clem said passionately, clutching my arm, "for the scholarship."

It turned out that he'd been awarded college funding, due to a city program that I had instigated. He was now a junior at Hunter College.

"If it wasn't for you, man, I'd be a construction worker like my old man. I'm gonna be a teacher."

The look on his face and the way he grabbed my hand and pumped it again were enough reward for all the mayor-bashing I'd endured over the years. Well, for most of it, anyway.

No sooner had Clem and the Mikes sidled away than the stage door opened and several chorus members emerged, dressed in street clothes. The rest of the cast began to trickle out in the next ten minutes, and I watched as minor characters signed *Playbills* and posed for pictures.

Kellie Farrell slipped out, greeted fans for a few minutes, and hopped into a cab. She hadn't seen me. Shortly after that, Wesley Fisk appeared. He didn't bother with the crowd, just bent his head and shoved his way through despite their protests. Since he never looked up, he wasn't aware of my presence either, which was fine with me.

I spotted Jonathan Patrelli, the understudy who had taken over the role vacated by Conor, signing autographs and looking edgy, I thought. He seemed anxious to get away.

I didn't let him. As soon as the cluster of people around him dispersed, I closed in with a handshake and introduction before he knew what hit him.

"It's a pleasure to meet you, Mr. Mayor," he said politely, looking as though it was anything but.

"Do you mind if I ask you a few questions, Mr. Patrelli?"

"Actually . . ." He glanced at his watch, then out at the street. "I'm in a hurry at the moment. I only have a few hours before I have to be back here for the evening performance, and I have to be someplace . . ."

"It would only take a few moments," I pressed.

"I'm sorry," he said over his shoulder, already heading for the street. "Some other time?"

I nodded, watching from beneath furrowed brows as he disappeared.

I would definitely get to him—and soon.

Finally, Lara Marie Landry came out. She was a lithe, lovely woman, simply dressed in jeans and a T-shirt. She had pink cheeks and sparkling eyes and a mass of curly brown hair. She took her time with the fans, asking them about themselves and making them feel as though they mattered. I was impressed.

When she finally started to head for the street, I caught up with her, tapped her on the shoulder, and said, "Miss Landry?"

She spun, looking startled, and raised her eyebrows when she recognized me. "Hello, Mr. Mayor," she said, shifting her shoulder bag to her other arm and offering her right hand.

"Would you mind if I asked you a few questions? We can go somewhere for a drink—or coffee," I added, remembering what Dan Marinowski had said about her not drinking.

"Coffee would be great," she said, breaking into a smile. "There's a deli around the corner. I was actually headed over there to grab something to eat before the next performance."

"Then I'll buy you dinner," I said, and fell into step beside her. "I saw you in the show last week. You were marvelous."

"Thanks," she said warmly. "The admiration is mutual. I've always been a fan of yours. I really admire what you've done for the homeless."

For the next few minutes, as we headed over to Seventh Avenue, we discussed politics and show biz. I liked her very much already, and decided instinctively that I wasn't questioning her as a suspect, but as a witness . . . although you never know.

"What did you want to talk about?" she asked, once we were settled at a table toward the back of a mostly deserted deli. She bit into the huge sour pickle that had been propped next to the thick corned beef sandwich on her plate.

I hadn't intended to order anything to eat, but had caved once I saw the menu. Still, what harm could be done by one measly mushroom knish with brown mustard? Not that the potato pastry on my plate was actually *measly*. It was one of those fluffy, round, golden-brown monstrosities you can only find in a real kosher deli.

I bit into it—delicious—and said, "Conor Matthews," knowing she already knew.

She nodded, looking sad. "What do you want to know about him?"

"What was your relationship with him?"

"We were friends . . . good friends," she added.

"So you knew him well."

I expected her to say that she had, but instead she shrugged.

"I don't know if anyone really knew Conor," she told me. "He was a very private person. There were things he didn't discuss, things that troubled him . . ."

"What kinds of things?"

"I'm not sure. I know that he wasn't completely sold on doing *The Last Laugh.*"

"Because he would have rather been doing Shakespeare?"

"Exactly." She sipped her flavored sparkling water. "Conor was trained at the Royal Shakespeare Company in London, Mr. Mayor. He lived to play Romeo, and Othello . . . not Quincy Tate."

"So you think that was making him unhappy."

"Not *just* that, no. But it was part of it, yes."

"What else bothered him?"

"I don't know, exactly," she said.

I knew, and sensed she did, too, that the subject of Kellie Farrell was hovering over us like Marley's ghost.

"Do you think," I asked Lara Marie carefully, "that Conor knew about Kellie and Wesley?"

The look that flashed over her face was surprise, followed by uncertainty. "I'm not sure," she said after a moment.

I've been in law and politics long enough to know when someone is holding back on me. Lara Marie Landry wasn't telling me something, and I informed her that I was fully aware of that.

Taken aback, she said, "I'd rather not discuss Conor's personal relationship with his fiancée, Mr. Mayor."

"I'm not crazy about poking my nose into a stranger's love life myself, Ms. Landry. But we're talking about a homicide, here."

For a moment she was subdued, and she put down her sandwich. Then she nodded, looked me in the eye, and said, "Conor knew."

"How do you know?"

"Because I told him."

I raised an eyebrow. "I see. Were you and Conor involved?"

"Romantically? No!" she said. "He was totally faithful to Kellie. He was that kind of man . . . very passionate, very committed to things he believed in. I know he believed in Kellie."

"So you told him what she was doing because . . ."

She sighed. "Because I thought he had a right to know that the woman he was going to marry was carrying on with someone else behind his back."

"Do you mind if I ask how you knew about Kellie and Wesley?"

"I saw them kissing in his dressing room one night. It was late, and I'd come back to the theater for my bag—I'd forgotten it. I saw them, but they didn't see me. I knew I had to tell Conor."

"When was this?"

"A few weeks ago."

"How did he react to the news?" I asked, picking up my knish again, not wanting to let it grow cold. There's something about cold potatoes that really isn't appetizing.

"He was really quiet at first," Lara Marie said, a faraway look on her face. "But I don't think he was shocked, or anything. It was almost as if he'd suspected it. Then he became angry. Furious, really. We were in his dressing room, and he picked up a crystal bowl some fan had given him, and I thought he was going to smash it on the floor."

"But he didn't."

"No. He just set it down—he was shaking all over—and told me to please leave him alone. So I did. And that was it."

"You never discussed it with him again."

"No."

"He never said any more about it."

She seemed edgy as she answered, "No, he didn't."

"And did you ever tell anyone about this?"

"No, I didn't," she said. "The cast is like a bunch of small town busybodies, Mr. Mayor. We work very closely together—too closely. People talk. Things get around. I didn't want Kellie or Wesley to know that I'd seen them and told Conor."

"Why not?"

She shook her head. I caught something fleeting in her eyes, something I couldn't identify. "What they were doing wasn't meant for anyone to see," she told me. "They thought they were alone. It was none of my business, I know . . ."

"But you told Conor because you cared about him."

"Very much," she said. Something in her tone, in the way she looked down at her clasped hands, told me that Lara Marie Landry might have been a little bit in love with Conor Matthews.

I wondered—very, very reluctantly—if she had been capable of killing him out of jealousy over his involvement with another woman. Stranger things have happened, and yet . . .

I didn't want to believe that this sweet woman could have been behind a cold-blooded murder. I *couldn't* believe it. And yet, I felt compelled to add her name to my mental list of suspects.

"Ms. Landry," I said. "Who had access to the gun that killed Conor Matthews?"

"Only Dan—he's the propertyman. And Teresa Jaffe, the stage manager. It was kept in a locked cabinet, and they had the only keys. Oh, and Wesley, of course. He had access because he was the one who used the gun onstage. . . ." She shuddered slightly.

"Could someone else in the cast—let's say, Kellie Farrell, or you—or even one of the crew members—could someone else have had an opportunity to tamper with the gun?"

"It wouldn't have been easy. The props are under lock and key. Unless, of course, Dan screwed up and forgot to lock the cabinet or keep an eye on the gun when it was in the wings during the second act."

"How likely would it have been that Dan might have done just that?"

She hesitated. "I hate to speak badly about anyone, Mr. Mayor, but Dan isn't exactly the most responsible person you ever met. Conor always said he partied way too much—of course, Conor wasn't very tolerant of drinking and drugs. . . ."

"So I've heard."

"Listen, don't get me wrong. I'm not crazy about that kind of thing either," she said. "I was raised in Utah—I'm a Mormon. I abstain from alcohol and drugs. But I don't necessarily have a problem with what other people do."

"Conor did have a problem with it, though."

"He frowned on members of the cast who drank and smoked dope, yes. He even . . . he lectured a few of them, from time to time."

"Including Dan?"

"He thought Dan was a lost cause. He told me that Dan used to sneak off to his car during the show, to smoke a joint. And that Dan was careless with the props."

"Who else knew that?"

"I don't know. I don't really think anyone else paid much attention. With Conor, it was almost—well, not a crusade, but . . ."

She trailed off, and I nodded that I understood.

"What do you think of Jonathan Patrelli?" I asked, switching gears again.

"Jonathan? He's all right," she said noncommittally.

"Just all right?"

"I don't really know him all that well," she said with a shrug. "But what I know, I like. He's turned in some good performances this week under an enormous amount of pressure."

I nodded.

"You don't think he's the one who killed Conor," Lara Marie said, her eyes widening.

"I didn't say that. Do *you* think he did?"

"No!"

"Why not?"

"Why would he?"

"To have a stab at stardom?" I suggested.

"That's such a cliché, Mr. Mayor—the understudy bumping off the leading man. Do people really believe that everyone in show business is that cutthroat?"

"Not *everyone*," I said. "But I would say that Jonathan Patrelli had a fairly logical motive, wouldn't you?"

"No," she said, shaking her head. "I can't see Jonathan doing such a horrible thing. He's a nice person. He hasn't even demanded to move out of the dressing room he shares with three other people, even though he was told he'll be getting Conor's dressing room, eventually."

"What's the holdup?"

"I heard that the police have asked that the dressing room, and everything else up there, be left as it was when the murder was committed. I guess they want to go through it, but they haven't come up with a search warrant yet, or something. My point is that Jonathan isn't exactly jumping to take over, the way you'd think someone would if they actually killed a person just to get a role."

I popped the last morsel of knish into my mouth and asked, point-blank, "Then who do you think *was* responsible for killing Conor?"

She blinked. "I don't know . . ."

"Come on, Ms. Landry. You must have a theory."

"I honestly have no idea," she said, looking down as though the crumpled straw wrapper in her hand were the most fascinating thing she'd ever seen.

I knew that she was holding back again.

"What aren't you telling me, Ms. Landry? Come on . . . this is between you and me."

She looked up, her brown eyes large and round. "What makes you think I'm not telling you something?"

"I'm the mayor," I said for lack of anything better.

She seemed to accept that. "Actually," she said, toying with the wrapper, "I've been thinking of calling that detective who spoke with me the first night—Rabinowitz, his name was."

"Yes," I said with a nod. "You spoke with him?"

"Only briefly. He talked to all of us in the cast, one-on-one. At the time, I was so shocked and upset that I didn't think to tell him . . ."

"Tell him what?" I prodded.

For a long time, she didn't respond.

Then she looked up at last and said, "For all I know, it doesn't mean anything. I don't want to get an innocent person into trouble . . ."

"Who is that person?" I asked.

She hesitated, then said, "Kellie Farrell."

I set down my seltzer can and leaned across the table. "What about her?"

"It's just something Conor said," Lara Marie told me, fiddling with a silver filigree ring she wore on her right hand.

"About Kellie?"

"Yes." She took a deep breath. "If it gets out—well, I'm afraid . . ."

"Afraid of what?" I asked. "Of whom?"

"Of Kellie," she said shakily. "You can't tell anyone what I'm going to say, Mr. Mayor. Not even the police."

"But—"

"Forget I said anything." Her mouth clamped shut and she looked around skittishly.

"No, no," I urged, "you can tell me. I promise I won't tell a soul."

Still, she faltered.

"I promise, Ms. Landry," I said again. "Go ahead."

"Conor told me, a few days after I let him know what she was up to, that he thought . . ."

"Thought what?" I asked, frustrated as I watched her biting her lip.

Finally, the words spilled out of her in a rush. "He thought she was trying to kill him."

_____TEN

I didn't feel so hot when I awoke on Sunday morning in my Greenwich Village apartment. I'd had an uncharacteristically restless night, marked by nightmares about Kellie Farrell chasing me through the Regal Theater with a bloody ice pick.

Luckily, a cup of steaming black Martinson's helped me feel a little less groggy, and a toasted bialy with chive cream cheese, capers, and Nova Scotia lox helped soothe my nerves.

I put the soundtrack to _The Last Laugh_ on the stereo and sat down in the living room with my third cup of coffee.

Lounging on the couch with my feet on the coffee table, I tried to read the _Times_. Instead, I found myself distracted by the music, humming along with the show's overture as it flooded my apartment, then singing every word to every song on the CD. The lyrics and melodies weren't as clever as Sondheim's, nor as sweepingly emotional as Lloyd Webber's, but they were catchy enough to stick in your mind. I had known them all by heart for years.

Conor Matthews must have been extremely agitated the night of his murder, I realized, in order to have flubbed so many lines— not just dialogue, but song lyrics, as well. After all, half the people in America know every word to the show's big hit, "Hug Me, Hugo." But as I recalled, Matthews had made several mistakes even in that number.

It was too bad, I thought wistfully, that I couldn't return to last Saturday night's performance, knowing what I now knew. It would be interesting to see whether Matthews was the only one who seemed noticeably uptight that night. I couldn't help wondering if Kellie Farrell had been as smooth as I recalled—or if maybe I'd missed something, as I hadn't been paying particular attention to her performance.

If only it were possible to go back in time . . .

I sat up on the couch so suddenly that I sloshed hot coffee all over my khakis.

Time travel might be impossible, I realized, but I *could* relive last Saturday night's performance.

It just so happens that last month at a banquet, I presented a humanitarian award, on behalf of the city, to Jacob Netherman— a well-known supporter of local charities, and handpicked for the honor by Yours Truly.

Jacob Netherman happens to be a senior vice president of programming at Chapman-Hart, the communications conglomerate.

And Chapman-Hart, of course, owns the premium cable television channel, Home Entertainment Network—which was videotaping the gala performance of *The Last Laugh,* to air as a special during the Christmas season.

Until now, I had somehow forgotten all about the fact that a tape had been made. I assumed it would no longer be shown on television, what with the tragic ending. But that didn't mean the videocassette had been destroyed . . .

Luckily, Jacob Netherman is a jovial guy who had no problem with being called at his home in Greenwich on a Sunday morning.

"Ed, what can I do for you?" he asked cheerfully, after his housekeeper had summoned him to the phone. I could hear a television blaring in the background.

"I'm sorry to interrupt whatever you were doing, Jacob . . ."

"Not a problem. I was just flipping around with my remote, waiting for the Jets game to start."

I was intrigued by the prospect of this man—who is responsible for much of what's on television—channel surfing. I wondered if he was sizing up the competition and making sure his own networks were up to par, or merely restlessly searching for temporary amusement, like the rest of us.

"It's probably way out of line for me to ask you this," I said, "but I need a favor. A big one."

Three minutes later, as the Jets game got underway, Jacob Netherman was, I presume, once more riveted to his television set.

And I was smiling at the prospect of receiving a copy of the videotaped gala performance, first thing in the morning at City Hall, via special messenger.

According to Charley Deacon, whom I reached by telephone at the precinct on Sunday evening, the investigation was going smoothly.

"The papers say you're about to make an arrest," I pointed out. "Is that correct?"

"Well," he hedged, "I'm hoping and expecting that we'll take someone into custody soon. But you and I both know we can't do anything without a warrant, and I can't just snap my fingers and produce one."

"Who's going to be arrested?"

"You know I can't give you that information."

"I know, but Charley . . ."

"Listen, I might as well let you know that Rabinowitz isn't comfortable with you infringing on his territory in this case, Mayor," Charley told me in a low voice. "I don't need him breathing down my neck on this end if he thinks I'm going around revealing things I shouldn't."

"You haven't revealed anything to me, Charley," I pointed out.

"Right. Because I can't," he said abruptly. "But how are things going on your end?"

"Fine." I wanted to tell him what I knew, but I couldn't, thanks to promises I'd made. There are a lot of politicians whose word is as good as Monopoly money, but when I say I'll do something, I mean it.

And so, I kept quiet about Kellie and Wesley's affair, and Conor Matthews's drinking, and his fear that Kellie was trying to do him in. Maybe if Rabinowitz were a less abrasive personality, the people he'd questioned would have been more forthcoming with him, as they had been with me.

And anyway, I told myself, if the police didn't solve the case in the next day or so, *I* would.

Either way, the killer—or killers—of Conor Matthews would be behind bars. And that was what mattered.

On Monday morning, the world was rainy and gray—not the best way to start a week, though I was optimistic and anxious to get down to business.

Traffic was snarled, thanks to a truck that had spilled a load of Grandma Goldstein's Bottled Borscht in midtown, smack in the center of Fifth Avenue. Luckily, I arrived at my office just in time to accept a call from the White House.

It seemed that the President and First Lady would be in town tomorrow to attend a reception at the U.N.

I like the President, although he clearly has major character failings, and have always gotten a kick out of his wife. She tells it like it is, a trait I've always admired in others—and been proud to possess myself.

And so, in between my usual round of Monday morning appointments, I set the wheels in motion to clear my Tuesday schedule in order to meet with the First Couple for breakfast. That took some juggling, as I'd already been scheduled to be five different places between nine and eleven, followed by an early lunch at a Brooklyn soup kitchen.

But Maria Perez, who was proving herself to be more efficient than Rosemary Larkin—something I'd never imagined possible—had everything under control by noon. She'd even lined up Hinda Grisin of Fab Affairs to cater the morning meal here at City Hall, requesting the President's favorite bacon and egg concoction, one that is loaded with butter and cheese. My mouth watered just thinking about it.

Talk about your hectic Mondays . . . I was swamped. It wasn't until my lunch arrived—takeout moo goo gai pan from Kung's—that I finally caught my breath . . . and remembered the videotape.

I poked my head out of my office and found Maria just hanging up the phone.

"I was expecting a package from Jacob Netherman of Chapman-Hart," I told her. "Did it—"

"Right here." She handed me a padded brown envelope. "I was just about to bring it in to you."

I thanked her and returned to my office, closing the door behind me. I turned on the television, popped the tape into the VCR, and settled in my low-slung black leather armchair, which is the most comfortable seat in my office. Before pressing Play, I opened the takeout carton and doused my lunch with soy sauce and hot mustard.

Then I started watching the taped performance of *The Last Laugh.*

I say *started* because I only got through the first half hour of the program before it was time to dash off to a meeting with the Deputy Mayor of Human Services and several financial advisors to discuss the proposed closing of two hospitals, one in Queens, the other in the Bronx.

As I headed down the hall to the conference room, I thought about what I'd seen on the tape. Conor Matthews was clearly agitated—even more so than I recalled.

It was difficult to watch his performance, knowing what was going to happen to him before the curtain came down on the final act. I was so disturbed, in fact, that I barely touched my lunch—I'd stashed the nearly full carton in the refrigerator in the kitchenette off to the side of my office.

As I conducted what turned out to be a volatile meeting, I found myself slightly preoccupied, haunted by the memory of Conor Matthews's troubled, almost dazed eyes—captured in close-up by a zoom lens more than once during the first two scenes.

It was almost as if the man had somehow suspected what was going to happen.

My decision to contact Richard Matthews, Conor's father, was made late Monday when I realized that I would be in New Jersey tomorrow afternoon. I was meeting with several representatives of the Metropolitan Transit Authority in Hoboken to discuss with New Jersey officials a proposed new high-speed commuter ferry service linking Hoboken with lower Manhattan.

And so, as long as I was going to be in the neighborhood . . .

"Hello, Mr. Matthews, this is Ed Koch," I said into the telephone, having tracked him down at the accounting firm where he worked via Maria, the wonder secretary.

"Ed Koch . . . the mayor?" he asked, sounding more than a little surprised.

"Yes. We met last week at . . ." I trailed off, unsure of how to put it delicately.

"At Conor's funeral. Yes, I remember." He waited, and I could almost picture him seated at his desk, nervously thrumming his fingertips on the desk.

"I'm going to be in Hoboken tomorrow afternoon," I said, "and I was wondering if you would have some free time at, say, sometime after four-thirty?"

He stammered that he thought he might be free, and asked why.

"Because I'd like to meet with you."

"With me?"

"Yes. I'd like to talk about your son . . ."

He sharply expelled a breath, and hesitated before saying, "Quite frankly, Mr. Mayor, I'd rather not discuss Conor. It's still very painful for me."

I wanted to say, quite frankly, *Bull.* His tone—and everything I'd noticed about him at the funeral—told me that he wasn't exactly a profoundly grieving parent.

If he had been, of course, I'd have left him alone. But under the circumstances, I pushed. Hard.

As a result, I hung up the phone only after having reached an agreement to meet with Matthews at his home. I'd suggested a restaurant, or even his office, but he'd insisted that I come to his house in Rutherford, where we could, as he put it, "have a drink and relax."

As it wasn't very far from Hoboken—and I was admittedly a bit curious about his lifestyle—I'd told him I'd see him there at five o'clock sharp.

Breakfast with the President. Lunch with the Homeless. Drinks with a Deadbeat Dad.

Tomorrow, it seemed, would be a typical day in the life of the mayor.

I didn't get home Monday evening until nearly eleven, thanks to a festive Rosh Hoshannah dinner sponsored by the American Jewish Committee at a loft space on Canal Street. It had been a delightful evening, filled with traditional food and drink reminiscent of the Jewish holidays of my childhood: tender brisket, sweet kosher wine, rich rugelach, and the customary apples with honey— symbolic of a sweet new year.

Though I hadn't slept well the past few nights, I wasn't the least bit drowsy when I got back to Gracie Mansion. The videotape had been in the back of my mind all evening, and as soon as I'd changed out of my suit, I settled in front of the television in my room to watch the rest of it.

Conor Matthews definitely seemed muddled; increasingly so as the show went on. Knowing about the alcohol he'd apparently consumed that evening, I found myself noticing the way he swayed a bit as he went through the intricate dance routines, and he seemed to slur a few of his lines—particularly when Wesley Fisk, portraying his nemesis Hugo Shields, was onstage.

For their parts, Wesley and Kellie appeared to be utterly professional, although I noticed Kellie's eyes widen a bit the first time Conor bent close to kiss her toward the end of the first act.

She had just sniffed the booze on his breath, I realized, playing the scene several times in slow motion. From that point on, though she performed her dialogue, lyrics, and dance steps flawlessly, there was something a little strained about her, especially when she was interacting with Conor.

When it came time for the big production number at the end of Act One, Conor Matthews was visibly bungling his way through. That, as you'll recall, was the scene where the vintage Packard is driven out onstage—a real showstopper. The song is "Hug Me, Hugo," sung by Quincy Tate to his supposed buddy, the devious Shields, who has just landed them their big break on the vaudeville circuit.

It was clear, after rewinding and studying the scene twice, that the last thing Conor Matthews wanted to do was sing Wesley Fisk's praises, much less throw his arms around him in a fervent bear hug. As he tap-danced his way around the stage and all over the car, flanked by his nemesis and the chorus, he barely seemed to be going through the motions. His lyrics were pretty garbled, and I wondered whether it was due to the liquor or his own animosity toward his costar.

Both, most likely.

Something was bothering me about that number, but I couldn't keep watching it over and over again. I still had an hour and a half of tape to watch, and I was starting to yawn despite my interest in the performance. It would hardly do for me to fall asleep in my eggs in the company of the President and First Lady, so I left "Hug Me, Hugo," behind and worked my way through the rest of the video.

As the final act wound toward a close, I found myself shuddering in anticipation of what was to come. And again, I sensed that Conor Matthews almost seemed to have a premonition of his own doom. He seemed subdued at times, then almost frantic during the scene where he discovers that Amber is two-timing him with Hugo.

The fury and emotion in his final solo were, of course, part of the scene. And yet, every muscle in his body, every note his voice struck, reverberated with fierce tension, sending chills down my spine.

When Hugo Shields confronted him with the gun, his character was supposed to be joking around—it was, after all, part of their act—the show within a show. And yet, there was a hollow note in Conor Matthews's voice as he forced a laugh, and though the camera didn't zoom in on his eyes, I could almost read the anxiety in them.

He's worried, I realized as he stared down the barrel of the revolver, daring Shields, in a shaky voice, to shoot him. *He's thinking that it would be so easy for life to imitate art.*

As the shots rang out, I winced, and pressed my hand against my mouth in renewed horror as I watched Kellie Farrell cradling him, then breaking into a frenzy as she realized what had happened.

I rewound and froze the frame on a close-up of her face, taken just before the tape dissolved abruptly into nothing.

Her mouth was open in a silent scream, her lovely face contorted into a mask of terror, her blue eyes round with shock . . . or so it seemed.

Kellie Farrell, I thought with grudging admiration, was the consummate actress. It was impossible to tell whether she was truly stunned and appalled as her fiancé's lifeblood trickled over her hands . . .

Or whether she was expertly hiding the fact that she'd known this was coming—that she had, indeed, engineered the tragic scenario.

I still, in my gut, believed that she was innocent. Or maybe it's just that I wanted to. My instincts, after all, had said to trust her. And my instincts are almost always right; in fact, I have relied on them, personally and professionally, all my life.

But there's a first time for everything, I conceded. Perhaps, for the first time, I was totally wrong about someone.

But I wasn't wrong about Richard Matthews. No, my first impression of him at the funeral last week proved to be right on target. The man was a cool S.O.B. whose indifference toward his son was obvious in everything he said and did.

I was over an hour late arriving at his house in Rutherford on Tuesday afternoon, which didn't exactly seem to thrill him. He opened the door looking more than a little put out, and made a point of glancing at his watch.

I apologized and explained that the President and First Lady were late for our breakfast, thanks to a noisy foreign policy protest that took place that morning in front of the midtown hotel where they were staying. Finally the Secret Service snuck them out safely, and they were most apologetic for their tardiness, knowing better than anyone that I'm a busy man.

As a result, my Tuesday schedule was completely thrown off, and there was nothing on the agenda that could be easily canceled in order to get me back on track. And even though I kept the Hoboken meeting, my final appointment of the day, as brief as possible, the traffic on the New Jersey Turnpike was horrendous and it took longer than it should have to get to Rutherford.

"It's always horrendous," Richard Matthews said tersely when

I explained. What could I do but shrug and decide I couldn't stand the man?

He invited me into his home, a beige raised ranch on a quiet cul de sac. It was an upscale suburban dream, all of it—from the Range Rover parked in front of the double attached garage to the scent of fresh cut flowers that greeted me as I stepped over the threshold.

Matthews wore khaki slacks, loafers, and a yellow polo-style shirt; the most casual outfit in the world, and he was acting anything but. He moved stiffly and reluctantly, and I knew that I was anything but welcome.

"Is your wife at home?" I asked, following him up a short flight of hardwood steps to a long living room that ended in a whole wall of stone fireplace. An in-ground pool and expensively landscaped yard were visible through double sets of French doors.

"No. She took Kimberly to her riding lesson," he said, motioning for me to sit on the puffy chinz couch.

"Kimberly?"

"My younger daughter," he said. "Kerry's the older one. She's at the mall with her friends, as usual."

I glanced at the row of framed photos on the mantel. There were several of the two girls at various stages, typical school portraits. And there was a large glamour shot of his wife, a stunning brunette who looked too young to have teenaged daughters. Nowhere, amidst the gallery of photographs, was there a picture of Conor.

"Can I get you a drink, Mr. Mayor?"

I noticed that Matthews looked uncomfortable, and wondered if he knew what I was thinking.

I asked for a glass of wine, something light and fruity, and he crossed over to a wet bar tucked into a corner by the fireplace. He poured a glass of blush for me and a single malt scotch for himself.

Finally, he was perched opposite me in an easy chair, looking at me guardedly over the rim of his glass.

"What is it that you wanted to ask me, Mr. Mayor?" he asked after taking a long swallow.

"I'm investigating your son's death, as you may know," I told him. He neither nodded nor shook his head; merely stared at me, waiting. "I thought you could tell me a little about him."

"About Conor?" He shook his head slightly, sipped again. "I can't tell you much of anything that you couldn't find out from interviews he's done over the years."

"Oh?"

"I didn't raise my son, Mr. Mayor," he said with more than a trace of bitterness. "My wife threw me out when he was young enough not to notice or care, after a few days, that I was missing."

"She threw you out? You didn't leave her?"

He shook his head grimly. "Mindy and I had our problems, but I never walked out. She ordered me to leave. So I did." He shrugged.

"Why did she throw you out?"

"I told you, we had our problems."

Sure they did. Her drinking; his philandering—at least, according to Sybil. I wondered if Mindy had discovered her husband was having an affair and tossed him out because of it.

After only a second's deliberation, I decided to come right out and ask him.

Richard Matthews's eyebrows shot up beneath the swoop of salt-and-pepper hair on his forehead. He cleared his throat and said so coldly that I knew I'd hit the nail on the head, "I don't think that's any of your business, and I don't see what it has to do with my son's murder."

"I apologize if I seem to be prying into your personal life, Mr. Matthews, but I want to investigate every angle of this case, and I need to understand what your son's past was like."

"As I told you earlier, Mr. Mayor, I have no idea. I had no connection with Conor after I left."

"Your choice, or his?"

"Pardon?"

"Who cut off contact, Mr. Matthews? Did you choose not to see your son, or did he choose not to see you?"

"His mother made the decision," he said. "I wasn't about to intrude on what she considered her territory. I wrote her off the day she told me our marriage was over."

"And your son, too."

He set his jaw. "My son was poisoned by what his mother told him. He hated me."

"Did you pay alimony and child support?"

He visibly flinched. "Of course I did . . . at first. But then I realized that Mindy was spending my money on booze, so I stopped."

"Did you ever try to see your son?"

"Yes!" he said defensively. "Quite a few times. Whenever I called, Mindy hung up on me. And I invited Conor to the wedding when I married Carole, but his mother wouldn't let him come."

"Carole . . . ?"

"My wife, obviously," he said, his own gaze shifting to the mantel.

"How did you meet her?"

"Work," he said shortly.

"When?"

"Look, I know what you're getting at, Mr. Mayor, so I'll tell you that yes, I did meet Carole while Mindy and I were still married. But no, she wasn't the reason our marriage fell apart. Mindy was an impossible woman to live with. I never saw anyone change so drastically. When I met her, she was gorgeous and happy, a real party girl. By the time she killed herself, she was a bitter, disheveled old wreck just like her old man before he died."

I blinked. "Excuse me?"

"She was a wreck," he repeated, shaking his head—not sadly, but angrily, and his tone was caustic. "Like her father. The old guy drank himself to death before he turned forty, just like Mindy did."

"But did you say she killed herself?"

"Of course she did."

That was news to me. "What happened?"

"Booze and Valium," he said. "A real killer combination."

"Didn't she die accidentally?"

"Not a chance," he told me. "She used to threaten she was going to do it while we were still married—and the first few times, I was really worried, I'll tell you. We'd have a fight, and she'd tell me she was through, that she wanted to get a gun and kill herself. Or that she was going to sit in the garage with the motor running, that kind of thing. Every time, she had a new scenario. It was like she was fascinated with it. At first, I really believed her. Every time I left for work, I thought I'd find her dead when I got home. Do you know what that was like for me, living with a nut case like that? I didn't need to find my wife hanging from one of my neckties in the attic, you know what I mean? But after awhile, I started realizing it was just talk. She just wanted attention."

"But she really did do it," I said, half amazed that he could speak so matter-of-factly about something as serious as a desperate woman's suicide threats—and the other part of me not surprised at all. Richard Matthews wasn't exactly the type of man you'd expect to start weeping sentimentally over his ex-wife's death.

"Years later, yeah, she did do it," he conceded with a shrug. "I guess she finally talked herself into it."

"How did it happen?"

"I told you, booze and pills. Conor found her on his bedroom floor when he came home from school. It was like she did it in his room to be sure he'd find her right away. She collapsed on top of his aquarium, wrecked the whole damn thing. Broken glass and dead fish everywhere."

"They were living in the Nicolays' guest house at the time?"

"Tetty and Sebastian? Yeah. But they were off traipsing around in Europe, so the cops called me. I was busy with an important client, but you know, I dropped everything and went right over there."

"That was big of you," I murmured, but my sarcasm sailed right past him.

"Damn right it was. Hadn't seen the kid in years, and do you believe that he didn't want anything to do with me? Even then! I handled everything for him, though. After all, I am his father . . . I *was* his father," he amended, and for the first time, I saw what may have been a fleeting flash of regret in his eyes.

"What did you handle?" I asked.

"I kept it out of the papers . . . you know, that it was a suicide. No one ever knew. I figured it would be embarrassing. Even though we'd been divorced a long time, Mindy still used my name. I was building my career back then, and I had a lot of business contacts in the area. I didn't need it getting out that my ex had killed herself."

"But how did you know for sure that it wasn't an accidental overdose?"

"She left a note," he said with a shrug, and drank more scotch.

"Addressed to Conor. He told the cops he found it up in his tree house or something."

I remembered what Tetty had said about the tree house having a little mailbox where Mindy Matthews used to leave notes for her son. The charming scenario took on a gruesome twist. I had no doubt that she must have left her suicide note there for him, knowing he would find it. "What did it say?"

"Basically, just goodbye. She told him she had suffered too much—that I had made her miserable. Can you believe that after all those years, she still had it in for me? And she said that she knew he was old enough to be on his own, that he'd be fine. It was pretty damn melodramatic . . . but then, so was she. No wonder the kid grew up to be an actor."

"What happened to the note?"

"The kid ripped it up and flushed it down the toilet," he said. "Just like that. The cops showed it to me, then gave it back to him. He went into the bathroom—we were thinking he wanted to read it again, in private—and then he flushed it. The cops weren't happy. I guess they figured it was evidence, you know. But it was just as well. Like I said, it mentioned me, and I didn't need that getting out."

"What happened to Conor after that?"

"Come on, Mr. Mayor. You've researched his life, haven't you? You don't need me to tell you where he went, what he did." He checked his watch, made a movement as if to stand up and end the conversation.

"Did you ask him to come and live with you?" I asked.

He hedged. "Carole was pregnant with Kimberly, and Kerry was just a toddler. We had our hands full. Besides, there was no room. We lived in a two-bedroom condo. And anyway," he continued, as though I'd been arguing with him, "Conor didn't want to live with me. I told you, my son hated my guts. Wouldn't speak to me, never thanked me for helping him out, nothing. He did what I told him to do, though. Kept it quiet . . . about his mother killing herself, you know. It wouldn't help his career any more than it would help mine. He didn't want people knowing he had a self-destructive nut case for a mother. The neighbors didn't know, Mindy's friends—if you could call them friends; I think they just felt sorry for her—none of them ever knew. As far as they were concerned, she drank so much her liver finally just gave out. That was enough of a scandal—the truth would have been a real fiasco."

I felt more sorry for Conor Matthews than ever. But, I conceded, it was probably a blessing that his self-absorbed father hadn't been a part of his life. A man like Richard Matthews cared only for himself. I pitied his beautiful second wife and two young daughters, and wondered if the nice house and riding lessons were worth it. Some people, sadly, didn't need any more than that.

Obviously, Mindy Matthews had.

And her son had lived with the fact that she had deliberately abandoned him. He'd locked it inside and carried on; maybe he'd even used the pain in his acting. But he'd never let it out, apparently; had never admitted it to anyone, maybe not even to himself.

I thought about what Kellie Farrell had said, about being afraid of Matthews. She'd said he had a dark side, that she felt as though he were capable of snapping.

Had he yelled at her, threatened her, unleashed all his pent-up rage when he'd discovered her affair? Had she, in return, fearing for her own life, gotten him out of the picture?

It was a compelling scenario, one that would have made sense if not for one thing . . .

I still found myself wanting to believe that my instincts about Kellie had been correct. My feeling that she was innocent had been so strong, so certain, that it was difficult for me to let that go and consider her, once again, the prime suspect.

Because of that nagging, faint doubt, I vowed to continue as I had originally planned; that meant checking out the remaining suspects on my list: Nolan MacDougall, Beau Walton, and Jonathan Patrelli.

ELEVEN

Wednesday, I was so caught up in city business that I didn't have a moment to spare for the Matthews case, though it hovered in the back of my mind as I bounced from one calamity to the next.

All hell seemed to have broken loose in Manhattan, from a subway derailment in Harlem—no one was seriously injured, thank God—to a giant, beet-colored stain smack-dab in the middle of Fifth Avenue, thanks to Monday's borscht spill. Naturally, the press conference I was holding to announce the opening of a new city-funded children's health clinic turned into a free-for-all.

First I was barraged with questions about who was at fault in the subway accident. Naturally, it seemed to most of the reporters in the room that I, being mayor, was to blame.

No sooner had I deflected that ridiculous accusation than someone shouted, "How do you plan to get those unsightly stains out of the concrete in time for Sunday's Fireman's parade, Mr. Mayor?"

To that, I could only say, with as straight a face as possible, "I suppose I'll have to call my mother and ask her. She always did a great job getting red horseradish stains off my good Sunday shirts."

That got a laugh . . . and, predictably, a tabloid headline the next morning that announced, "Mayor's Mom to Share Stain-Removal Secrets."

Thursday, by contrast, was relatively quiet. Lillian Koch, presumably, hadn't heard about the borscht debacle or her own role in it, because there were no panicky ship-to-shore phone calls. My office was surprisingly quiet, my meetings went like clockwork, and I actually managed to leave just after six-thirty.

Finding myself with a free evening, I decided to kill three—hopefully, four—birds with one stone. After all, I'm a busy man. I don't have time to traipse all over town tracking people down to interrogate them. Why not simply show up at the one place where I was sure to find most—maybe even all—of my remaining suspects: The Regal Theater.

Besides, I knew it would be a good idea to sit through another performance of *The Last Laugh*. Maybe I'd pick up on some detail I'd missed.

Being mayor, I was able, with a few well-placed phone calls, to make arrangements for a prime house seat at the last minute, even though the show was sold out. And so there I was, taking my seat in the fifth row, center, just as the curtain went up on Act One.

I have two things to say about Thursday evening's performance. One is that it was smoothly executed, with not a missed cue, not a botched line . . . at least, not as far as I could tell. The cast members were flawless, including Kellie Farrell, Wesley Fisk—and Jonathan Patrelli in the role Conor Matthews had abandoned.

The second thing I have to say was that as I sat there watching the show, I couldn't help feeling as though there was something I should be remembering—something about Conor Matthews's last performance.

When the lights came up at intermission, I saw Nolan MacDougall and Beau Walton, both of whom had been seated a few rows in front of me, on the aisle, jump up and hurry toward the stage door. Good. They were both in attendance, as I had hoped. I would question them, and Jonathan Patrelli—not to mention the stage manager, Teresa Jaffe, if she was willing—as soon as the performance was over.

But for now, I stayed put. For one thing, I didn't have any interest in mingling with any of my friends or foes who were sure to be in attendance. I was too preoccupied to make small talk; too busy trying to remember whatever it was that kept eluding me.

For another thing, the less obtrusive my presence, the better, as far as I was concerned. The whole world might know I was investigating the Matthews case, but that didn't mean I had to broadcast my being at the theater.

Besides, I could swear I had glimpsed Detective Rabinowitz peeking out from the wings just before the first act had ended. It may just have been my imagination, but I wasn't in the mood for a confrontation.

The intermission seemed unusually long, and I soon became aware that it wasn't just because I was sitting staring at the curtain instead of sipping wine at the mezzanine bar. Most of the audience had returned to their seats without being summoned by the traditional dimming of the lights, and people were beginning to buzz.

Unfortunately, there was no one I could turn to and ask, "What do you think is causing the delay?" When I'd first been seated, I'd been pleased to see that I was sandwiched between two Japanese businessmen who spoke no English, and a hand-holding college-age couple so absorbed in each other that they didn't realize they were sitting next to the mayor. The foursome of elderly women in front of me never turned around, and behind me was a group of tourists with southern accents, also oblivious to my identity.

Ironic that for once, I was able to enjoy relative anonymity in a crowd . . . the one time I wouldn't have minded being engaged in the idle speculation upon which I was eavesdropping.

I considered finding my bodyguards, who were, of course, stationed around the theater, and asking them to find out what was going on backstage. But before I could do so, there was a crackling sound, like speakers coming to life.

Sure enough, a moment later a booming announcement was made.

"Ladies and Gentlemen, if I could have your attention, please . . . Your attention, Ladies and Gentlemen." Pause, while the audience settled down. "Due to sudden illness, Miss Kellie Farrell will not be continuing as Amber Blue in Act Two. The role will be played by Miss Farrell's understudy, Miss Toni Gatto. Thank you, and please do enjoy the remainder of the show, which will resume in approximately fifteen minutes. Please remain in your seats."

Immediately, the theater erupted in murmuring that swiftly

grew and became amplified. Everyone, it seemed, wanted to know what could possibly have happened to the leading lady, who had appeared perfectly healthy and robust only minutes earlier as she belted out a soulful solo.

Though I shared that curiosity with the rest of the audience members, there was a difference. They were forced to sit and gossip and wonder. I, on the other hand, being mayor, was able to summon my bodyguards and get to the bottom of things.

Thanks to Mohammed and Lou, I was able to get backstage in two minutes flat. Naturally, I was recognized as I edged my way out of my row and down the aisle. I simply smiled, nodded, and waved in response to the questions and comments from the audience.

The moment we stepped through the door and into the corridor that ran alongside the stage, we were plunged into chaos. Cast and crew members, theater personnel, and security guards mingled, some of them chattering excitedly or looking anguished; others trying to restore order.

I spotted a distraught Nolan MacDougall huddled with a uniformed NYPD officer. They appeared to be arguing, as both were using lots of hand gestures.

Flanked by my bodyguards, I headed in their direction and arrived just as the officer said, "Well, I'm sorry, Mr. MacDougall, but I told you, there's nothing *I* can do about it, and anyway, it's too late now, isn't it?"

With that, the cop turned away, and MacDougall's gaze fell on me.

"Mr. Mayor! What are you doing here?" he asked—somewhat suspiciously, I thought.

I ignored his question and posed one of my own. "What's going on? What happened to Kellie Farrell?"

He threw his hands up in the air, shaking his head. "I really can't believe he did this to me. Toni Gatto has been battling laryngitis all week. She's not strong enough to sing Amber Blue tonight, even for half an act. If only he had waited—"

"Who did what to you? If who had waited?" I persisted.

"That fat detective," he spat out, starting to turn away, his eyes distracted. "Rabinowitz. And his partner, Swanson."

So it hadn't been my imagination. I grabbed his sleeve. "What about them, MacDougall?"

He spun around just long enough to say, "They just arrested Kellie for the murder of Conor Matthews, that's what!"

Rabinowitz and Swanson had left with Kellie Farrell, but I found Charley Deacon by the door that led to the alley, giving orders to a few uniformed police officers.

When he was through, he turned, wearing a grim expression, and his gaze fell on me.

"Hello, Mayor," he said with a weary-looking nod.

"Can I have a word with you, Charley?" I asked in a low voice. "Privately?"

He looked reluctant. "I've got my hands full here . . ."

"You must have a minute," I pointed out, looking around and seeing that things seemed under control. The show had resumed— I could hear the opening lines of Act Two echoing faintly from the stage.

Charley sighed. "All right. We can slip into one of those offices over there."

I followed him—and my bodyguards, of course, followed me— to a tiny cubicle that was cluttered with boxes, file folders, and piles of papers that appeared to have no particular order. The desk and both chairs were stacked high with stuff, so we stood—not that Charley was likely to sit and take his time talking to me, anyway. He was definitely edgy, and his eyes kept darting toward the glass window in the closed office door, monitoring the activity on the other side.

"What happened?" I demanded.

"Didn't you hear? We arrested Kellie Farrell," he informed me calmly.

"I *know* that. Why?"

"Because she killed Conor Matthews."

"How did you arrive at that conclusion?"

"I told you once before, Mayor, this isn't my investigation. At least, I'm not the one who was in charge, here. But trust me when I say that there is considerable evidence against her. Enough to have gotten an arrest warrant issued."

"What evidence?" It wasn't that I thought Rabinowitz or the NYPD would make an arrest without sufficient reason. It was just that I had been so close to being certain of Kellie Farrell's innocence. Emotionally, I couldn't quite accept her guilt, though intellectually, I knew it was inevitable. I just couldn't believe I had been led so far astray by my own intuition.

"We found letters," Charley said after a moment's hesitation. "From Matthews. In her dressing room. And we found a journal that he kept, in his. Everything pointed to the fact that she had threatened to kill him, that he was terrified that she would. She had even attempted it on two separate occasions, according to his journal."

My jaw dropped. "You're kidding."

"I'm not. And the only reason I'm telling you is that this'll be all over the papers in the morning, anyway. The letters were reportedly leaked to the press this afternoon. I'm not sure about the journal. Probably that, too."

"What, exactly, did they say?"

"I told you," Charley said impatiently. "He was afraid she was going to kill him. He wrote to her repeatedly, begging her to forgive him for something that wasn't specifically mentioned. He also wrote, in his journal, that he suspected her of putting poison into his soda before a performance one night—he had supposedly caught her in his dressing room, slipping something into it. And he wrote that he'd awakened one night after they'd quarreled to find her standing over him clutching a pillow, as if she were about to smother him with it. According to his journal, she'd fallen apart, hysterical, and admitted that she'd meant to kill him."

I frowned, not quite able to envision the poised young woman behaving so erratically. I remembered what she'd told me about smelling liquor on Conor's breath, and how she suspected that someone had spiked his soda. Had she said it to throw me off her own trail? Had she been the one who'd slipped something into his drink . . . something far more volatile than liquor?

But if she'd gone that far, why bother using a gun to kill him?

Had she, perhaps, wanted to sedate Matthews so that he wouldn't be fully alert when the gun went off?

None of it made sense, and yet there it was, staring me in the face. Kellie Farrell had been arrested, and the police had evidence of her guilt.

"Were the letters and the journal the only basis for her arrest?" I asked Charley.

He paused so significantly that I knew there was more. "Actually," he said, "when we searched her dressing room we found a stash of soft-point bullets. They were hidden in a compartment inside one of those fake hair spray cans."

I knew what he meant. Pop has my great-grandmother's ruby ring and some other antique jewelry hidden inside a false tomato soup can in the kitchen cabinet. My mother yells at him about it once a week. She makes grilled cheese sandwiches and tomato soup every Sunday for lunch, and she's always trying to open that can before figuring out it's the imposter. Even I told Pop to get a safe-deposit box like a regular person, but he insists that it's safer "where I can keep an eye on it . . . Besides, who would ever think to look for jewels in a can of soup?"

The NYPD, obviously, since they'd managed to find bullets in a can of hair spray. It was hard to believe that Kellie would be careless enough to let the police find them, but then I guess she, like Pop, thought her hiding place was impenetrable.

"Did Kellie confess?" I asked Charley, and wasn't surprised when he told me that she hadn't. She didn't strike me as the sort who would fall apart under pressure, under any circumstances.

"They took her out of here by force, and the whole way, she was protesting that she was innocent," he said, and commented, "I'm surprised the other actors weren't so rattled by all this that they couldn't go back onstage. It was some scene, and it seemed to catch everyone off guard."

"They're professionals," I said with a shrug. "The show must go on. Incidentally, where's Wesley Fisk?"

"I have no idea. Onstage, I'd assume. Why?"

"He wasn't arrested?"

"No."

"He wasn't an accomplice, according to Conor's letters?"

There was a rap on the door right then. A uniformed officer

stuck his head in and told Charley he was needed immediately. It seemed that Nolan MacDougall wanted to see him, still demanding an explanation.

"We'll talk later, Mayor," Charley said, clearing his throat and heading for the door.

"I'd like to speak to Kellie Farrell, Charley," I said.

"You know you can't. At least, not now. She's down at the station, being interrogated by Rabinowitz and Swanson. Anyway, why do you want to see her now that we've got her in custody? The case is closed, and we appreciate your help," he added before disappearing into the corridor.

"Anytime," I said, still trying to shrug off that nagging shred of doubt.

Not doubt in Kellie Farrell's guilt. At least, I told myself that I couldn't doubt that. The evidence against her was significant.

No, it was self-doubt—something no mayor can afford. I have to be able to rely on myself, on my instincts, on my ability to judge people and situations. But for the first time, that sense seemed to have failed me, and I was left shaken to the core.

I was lying awake in my bed at Gracie Mansion, staring at the digital clock on the nightstand flip closer to midnight, when the intercom rang.

"I'm sorry to disturb you, Mr. Mayor," my housekeeper said nervously, "but there's an urgent call for you."

My thoughts darted to my parents. Every once in a while, you hear about a fire or accident involving a cruise ship. Had something happened to them?

"Put it through," I said a little hoarsely, telling myself that Bernie and Lillian Koch were undoubtedly safe and sound, probably complaining and bickering with each other right this very moment at a midnight buffet somewhere in the Caribbean.

More likely, this was some emergency involving the city. I hoped to God it wasn't another police officer shooting. Just last month, I had been summoned to Mount Sinai where a young rookie lay near death after being mortally wounded trying to make an arrest in front of a crack house. It happened too often, and I felt sickened at the thought of it.

But thankfully, that wasn't why my phone was ringing in the middle of the night. Not this time.

A familiar, low-pitched female voice that greeted me when I picked up the receiver.

"Mr. Mayor?" she asked, sounding a little hoarse. "This is Kellie Farrell. I assume you know where I am."

I sat up straighter in bed and said, "I certainly do."

"Please don't hang up on me."

"Why would I do that?"

"Because you believe I'm guilty, just like they do?"

"Are you?"

"No!" she said vehemently. "Mr. Mayor, I was telling the truth the other day when I told you I was innocent. You said you believed me. Please don't change your mind, and don't hang up on me. I swear I didn't kill Conor Matthews."

"I understand that the police have evidence that you did just that."

There was a moment of silence on the line. I didn't expect her voice, when she spoke again, to be strong and controlled, but it was.

"Mr. Mayor," she said, "I am being framed. Someone set me up. My lawyer believes that. My parents believe that. Why can't you?"

I paused, contemplating what she was saying. If I listened to my head, I'd wish her luck and hang up. But if I heeded my deepest instincts . . . I'd at least give her a chance.

It didn't seem likely that someone could go through such an elaborate scheme to frame her. In order to do so, someone would have to forge Conor Matthews's journal and letters to her . . . and plant the bullets in her dressing room.

It was possible, of course . . .

But hardly likely.

And yet, what if there was the slightest chance that she was telling the truth?

What if an innocent woman, a woman with a promising career and her whole life ahead of her, went to prison for a crime she didn't commit?

"Why are you calling me?" I asked cautiously, finally.

"Because you're the most powerful man in New York City," she said promptly. "And you said you were on my side. You've got to help me now. You've got to find the real killer, Mr. Mayor. He's out there somewhere, and he's dangerous. Who knows what he's capable of doing next?"

I contemplated that.

"Have you spoken to Wesley?" I asked her.

"No," she snapped. "It was difficult enough to be granted three phone calls. One was to my lawyer, one to my parents in Terre Haute, and one—"

"Yes, I know. Does that mean you think Wesley might have something to do with your being in prison?"

"I have no idea who's behind this, Mr. Mayor. But if it's Wesley, so help me God . . ."

"I've got a busy day tomorrow, Kellie," I told her after a moment's contemplation. "But I'll come to see you as soon as I can make arrangements. On one condition."

"What is it?"

"That you tell me everything you know about this case. *Everything.*"

"I already did!" she protested, starting to sound whiny, which wasn't at all becoming and not her usual style.

"Perhaps there were some details that slipped your mind. Or maybe there was something you thought wasn't important at the time, but—"

"Look, Mr. Mayor," she interrupted, back in control. "I told you everything. If Wesley had anything to do with this, his involvement completely escaped me. There was nothing that he said or did that indicated he might have it in for Conor, or that he was going to frame me. I'm not going to tell you anything different, and I'm not going to suddenly change my story to the police, or confess. I'm innocent. I didn't kill him, and I don't know who did. Do you believe me?"

I almost told her that I did. I *wanted* to tell her that.

And yet, I couldn't say it. Not this time.

What I said was, "I'll do what I can to discover the truth, Kellie. And I'll be in to see you. Now, it's late. You're going to need all your wits about you in the next few days, so try to get some sleep."

I did my best to take my own advice, but it was another long, restless night.

TWELVE

I had several messages from Sybil while I was in a conference Friday morning with my deputy mayors. That was followed by a consultation with the Fifth Avenue Association regarding the repaving of the short stretch of Fifth Avenue. It turned out not to be necessary: Manhattan's heavy traffic had quickly erased every trace of borscht. By the time I got in touch with Sybil, she was just leaving for a press luncheon at the Algonquin.

"I was calling for the exclusive you promised me," she said hurriedly. "When do you want to meet and chat?"

"Not until the case is closed," I informed her, in a rush myself, as I had arranged to see Kellie Farrell and I was supposed to be uptown in twenty minutes for our appointment.

"What do you mean? The case *is* closed. Kellie Farrell was arrested last night. Don't tell me you haven't heard!"

"I've heard."

"You promised to give me an exclusive on your investigation, Ed. I know you're a man of your word, so don't—"

"Sybil," I cut in, "I'm still tying up some loose ends on the Matthews case. When they're resolved, I'll talk."

"What loose ends?" she asked, sniffing out a possible scandal.

"I can't discuss them now. Just trust me when I say that there's more to this case than meets the eye."

She grumbled, but agreed to take my word for it before we hung up and dashed off to our respective appointments.

I met with Kellie Matthews in a small, dingy, windowless room the drab backdrop only making her seem more beautiful, more tragic. Her blond hair, pulled back into a simple ponytail, seemed as lustrous as ever, and her eyes were still a startling shade of blue, their expression not one of dejection, but of indignation and ire.

"You have to get me out of here, Mr. Mayor," she said as soon as we sat down on opposite sides of a small table, a stone-faced matron keeping watch over the prisoner.

"Tell me what you know, Kellie."

"If you ask me that one more time . . ."

I sighed, shook my head, and made a move as if to leave, and she said, "Wait! Wait, don't leave."

"If I'm going to help you, I need to know everything."

"But I've told you everything," she insisted, and again, I found myself inclined to believe her.

"If you didn't kill him, someone set you up," I said. "Who would have done something like that?"

"I've given that a lot of thought," she told me, "and Mr. Mayor, I honestly don't know. I want to give you an answer, but I just can't. I know that several people *could* have possibly had motives to want Conor dead—"

"Like who?"

"You know as well as I do. Beau Walton. Nolan MacDougall. Even Jonathan, I suppose . . . Or Wesley," she added reluctantly.

"Do you think one of those people is guilty?"

"No. I mean, even if one of them had killed Conor, why would they set me up? What do any of them possibly have against me?"

I stated the obvious. "It may not be that anyone has anything against you, Kellie. A lot of people know you were seeing Wesley behind Conor's back, which would give you a motive to get Conor out of the picture—"

"But I didn't—"

"Kellie, I'm operating under the assumption that you're innocent, as I told you. But you have to understand that you, as

Matthews's cheating fiancée, are one of the most likely suspects. The real killer would be aware of that, and framing you would naturally deflect suspicion away from the guilty person."

"Someone would have to hate me as much as he hated Conor in order to do that to me," she said, her voice hollow.

I shrugged, knowing what she was thinking. That Wesley may have been behind the whole thing—and if he was, she had been a fool to have trusted him.

Just as Conor Matthews was a fool to have trusted her.

I glanced at my watch. "I can't stay much longer, Kellie. Is there anything you want me to know?"

"Nothing except that I'm trusting you to help me, Mr. Mayor. And I have one of the best defense lawyers in town."

She was right about that.

Her attorney, Amanda Filbert, and I are old acquaintances. I've always admired her courtroom skills, though I haven't necessarily been happy with some of the clients she's represented over the years. She defended Andrew Steck, the notorious SoHo serial killer, a few years back, and managed to get him off on insanity. She's a legal powerhouse whose name is in the papers more often than not, as she usually takes high-profile cases. It didn't surprise me one bit when I read in this morning's papers that she'd be defending Kellie Farrell. This was right up her alley.

I made a mental note to call Amanda as soon as I had a chance. I was positive she was savvy enough to have a few tricks up her sleeve.

It wasn't until Friday evening that I was able to spare another few minutes for Kellie and the Matthews case. After my last meeting of the day—a session with my financial advisors to prepare for next week's budget meeting with the governor in Albany, and it didn't go particularly well—I managed to get in touch with Amanda Filbert.

"I've been expecting your call, Mr. Mayor," Amanda said in her usual brusque manner.

"I want to discuss Kellie Farrell's case, Ms. Filbert," I said, cutting straight to the point. Neither of us had time for beating around the bush. She would be preparing for tomorrow's arraignment, and I had to change into a tuxedo and be at a library benefit by seven-thirty.

"She's being framed, Mr. Mayor. And please call me Amanda."

"You can call me Ed," I said in return, then asked, "by whom?"

"One possibility is Wesley Fisk, though I think my client is reluctant to believe that. And I have reason to think that although he may be the most obvious choice, he may not be the guilty party. There are several other persons who were close to Mr. Matthews who are likely suspects. Or, of course, the murderer could have been a crazed fan."

"Would a crazed fan have been capable of setting up Kellie Farrell in such an elaborate scheme?"

"One never knows. I'm having the handwriting in those journals and letters analyzed by an expert."

"To see if they were forged?"

"Of course. Another thing—there were fingerprints found on the gun that don't match Kellie's."

"Well, other people handled it during the course of the production. Wesley Fisk, obviously, for one."

"He wears gloves in the scene where he shoots Quincy Tate," she pointed out. "His prints wouldn't be on the gun."

"And were they?"

"No."

That didn't mean he wasn't guilty, I thought. He could have worn gloves when inserting the deadly bullets. "Did you check out the properties manager?" I asked.

"Dan Marinowski? Yes, his prints were there. Nothing unusual about that. But like I said, the investigators found another set, and I want to know whose they are. No one else should have handled that gun."

"What about the stage manager?"

"Teresa Jaffe? We already had that checked out. The prints we found aren't hers. My guess is that they belong to the killer."

I nodded. "When do you expect to hear from the handwriting expert?"

"By Tuesday at the latest, but probably much sooner."

"What if the letters really were written by Matthews?" I asked.

"Circumstantial. That doesn't prove that my client committed the murder."

"And the bullets found in her dressing room?"

"Someone planted them there. Those dressing rooms weren't locked. Anyone could get into them."

I nodded, remembering what Wesley Fisk had said about seeing Conor sneaking out of Kellie's dressing room. Had he been lying to protect himself somehow? Did he want to reinforce the implication that Matthews was suspicious of Kellie, that he was, most likely, searching her things to find evidence that she was trying to kill him?

Or was Wesley telling the truth? Had Matthews really been paranoid about Kellie? Had Kellie really killed him?

There was no way of knowing.

Not yet.

I spoke with Amanda Filbert for as long as I could, keeping an eye on my watch. She agreed that Nolan MacDougall, Beau Walton, and Jonathan Patrelli all had possible motives and opportunity to want Matthews dead, just as I had originally concluded.

As for why any of them might frame Kellie Farrell, that was simple, just as I'd told Kellie. She was the most obvious candidate. Anyone who knew about her affair with Wesley Fisk—and apparently, there were few people in New York who didn't—would have to realize that she had a plausible motive to kill him. Had someone taken advantage of her romantic indiscretions?

Amanda's professional responsibility was only to cast reasonable doubt that Kellie Farrell had actually killed Conor Matthews. Mine, on the other hand, was to find out who had committed the bloody crime.

I didn't want that despicable villain walking the streets of my city.

And so, as Amanda went back to her work and I headed uptown in my limo, I was filled with renewed determination to continue the investigation and question the remaining suspects.

On Saturday morning, I took the Number One train up to Times Square. It was raining and cabs were scarce, so I put up my umbrella and walked the few blocks over to the Regal Theater.

The box office just inside the lobby was open, and there was a short line. The young man behind the glass cage didn't notice my entrance, and there was no one else around to stop me when I quickly slipped toward the back of the lobby and, after trying several doors, found one that was unlocked.

I was in luck, because as soon as I'd slipped through it, I found myself facing a stairway leading up. The floor above, I knew, was where the cast's dressing rooms were located.

It was remarkable, really, how easy it was for me, an outsider, to invade this supposedly off-limits part of the theater. If I could do it, so could someone else. Someone whose intent was to murder one person . . . and frame another.

Could the real killer have been someone not involved with the production after all? Could someone have walked in off the street, just as I had, and planted both the evidence and the bullets that eventually killed Conor Matthews?

The answer to both questions, of course, was Yes. But who?

My thoughts slid to Richard Matthews. Was there more to his connection with his son than I'd originally thought? Did the man have a reason to want Conor dead?

Cold and uncaring as Conor's father had seemed, I didn't want to believe that a parent could be responsible for the tragic death of his own child. And yet I knew that it wasn't entirely out of the question in this case.

Still, it was more likely that the killer had been a part of the production—or someone who longed to be a part of it. Like Beau Walton. I resolved to stick with my original suspects, at least for the time being.

I made my way down the deserted hallway, scanning the row of closed doors labeled with actors' names until I reached the one that read CONOR MATTHEWS.

An eerie sensation crept over me as I swiftly pushed the door open, stepped inside, and closed it behind me.

I turned on the light and saw . . .

Nothing.

Nothing unusual, that is.

I've been inside my share of Broadway dressing rooms, having gone backstage after performances to greet actor friends. This one was larger than some, smaller than others. I saw that it had the usual amenities: two chairs, a small table, a clothing rack, a full-length mirror, and a makeup mirror. It also had a small mini-refrigerator. There were some books on a shelf by the door. Several scripts lay on a low table by a chair beneath a reading lamp. A wilted philodendron sat on the narrow windowsill.

The walls displayed two medium-size posters—generic urban scenes, the kind you could buy cheaply in one of those open-front boutiques on St. Mark's Place or Bleecker Street. On the ledge below the mirror, amidst a clutter of grooming supplies, was a framed picture, a professional head shot of Kellie Farrell, the only remotely personal touch in the room.

Hmm.

I opened the refrigerator.

In it were two six-packs of Mountain Dew, a few bruised apples, and a white cardboard carton that appeared to be takeout Chinese and was probably responsible for the spoiled smell emanating from the fridge, which I quickly closed.

I moved to the shelf and glanced over the spines of the books that sat there. *The Great Gatsby*, a dog-eared biography of Ernest Hemingway, and a collection of poems by Sylvia Plath. So Conor hadn't been the type who read bestsellers or modern genre fiction . . . hardly a surprise.

On the ledge beneath the mirror, I saw a typical assortment of men's toiletries: shaving cream and a comb and brush and various hair gels and sprays, as well as his stage makeup.

The clothing rack was empty except for a maroon windbreaker, a few casual pairs of slacks and jeans, and a couple of shirts. Sneakers sat on the floor beneath the rack, as though the wearer had casually kicked them off and left them there.

The stack of scripts contained several Shakespearean tragedies, as one would expect. Yet toward the top of the stack were two contemporary plays: *'Night, Mother* and *Crimes of the Heart*. Was Matthews considering auditioning for a new production? I wondered. It didn't seem likely that he'd leave *The Last Laugh* for something other than a Shakespearean play.

I made a mental note to call Matthews's agent, Artie Masters, on Monday, and ask him about that. I'd thought of questioning him before, to see whether he had any ideas of who might want to kill his client, but I had been reluctant to contact him.

Masters is a notorious gossip, and I wasn't eager to get entangled with him unless it was absolutely necessary. He had been giving interviews to the press and appearing on tabloid television shows ever since the murder, lamenting the loss of his "number-one client" and generally doing his best to make it seem as though he were privy to Matthews's deep, dark secrets, though it was obvious that he had nothing to reveal. All I needed was for him to announce to the press that he'd joined forces with the mayor to nab Matthews's killer.

I glanced around the dressing room again, to see if there was anything I'd missed. Some actors tended to turn them into homes-away-from-home, filling them with personal touches and belongings. Conor Matthews didn't seem to have done that. I hadn't discovered anything earth-shatteringly significant about his private life in snooping through his dressing room. There were no boxes of fan letters or family photographs, no mementos from other shows or even knickknacks.

It wasn't until I'd closed the door behind me and started down the hall that I realized something important.

The fact that there *hadn't* been anything remotely intimate—aside from the photo of Kellie Farrell—in his dressing room was significant, in and of itself.

Why would a man who didn't even keep many personal belongings there, actually leave his private journal where anyone could find it?

I was walking down Broadway toward the subway station, lost in thought and hidden from the world beneath my umbrella, when a familiar face in the crowd jarred me to awareness.

"Jonathan?" I called, turning and catching up to the young man who'd just strode by me after emerging from the stairway leading to the train.

"Yes?" Jonathan Patrelli frowned slightly as he recognized me. He was wearing a pullover raincoat—bright red, which was why he'd caught my eye in the first place. He'd left the hood down as though he didn't care that his short, dark hair was getting soaked.

"I'm Ed Koch," I said unnecessarily.

He nodded and shook my hand, introducing himself politely though it was obvious that I knew who he was.

"On your way to the theater?" I inquired.

He hesitated, then said, "I was going to stop by a friend's apartment a few blocks away first. We have a matinee, but I don't have to be there for another hour."

"Do you have time for a cup of coffee with me?"

He looked as though he didn't. But one of the great things about being mayor is that some people seem to assume an invitation from Yours Truly is a command.

"A quick cup," Jonathan conceded, checking his watch. I wondered where he was in such a hurry to be. Something told me he was lying about visiting a friend.

We headed to the same deli where I'd eaten with Lara Marie Landry and found a secluded table in back. This time, I ordered only coffee, and Patrelli did the same. Judging by the way his hands shook slightly as he dumped two sugars into the cup, this wasn't his first cup of the day. Either that, or he was nervous about the prospect of talking to me.

Of course, as a famous person, I'm used to most people being a little intimidated in my presence. But I had a feeling that Jonathan Patrelli's jitteriness had nothing to do with the fact that I was the mayor of New York.

He sipped his coffee and waited for me to start talking. I noticed that the table was vibrating slightly and realized he was anxiously tapping his foot on the floor beneath it.

"I just wanted to see what you thought about the Matthews case, Mr. Patrelli," I said by way of an opening.

"What I *thought* about it?"

"Yes. For example, do you think Kellie Farrell is guilty?"

"She was arrested, wasn't she?"

"That isn't what I asked you. I didn't say, 'Was Kellie Farrell arrested?', I said, 'Do you think she's guilty?' Do you?"

"I have no idea," he said, his eyes shifting from mine to dart around the room. He gulped coffee that was apparently too hot, because he winced and quickly set the cup down, sloshing it over onto his fingers, which he hastily wiped on a napkin.

"What did you think of Conor Matthews?"

"He was all right," he said, "but he mostly kept to himself."

"Did you get along with him?"

"Sure. I get along with everyone. I like everyone in the show, you know?"

I nodded. "So you had nothing to do with Conor Matthews's death."

For the first time, I had his full attention. His eyes fastened on mine and widened in shock and horror. "No way! You think *I* killed him?"

"I didn't say that . . ."

"Oh, man. I can't believe you think I killed the guy. Why would I do a thing like that?"

I shrugged and again reminded him that I hadn't said he had.

"I know, but the way you're looking at me . . . Listen, Mr. Mayor, I wish I could help you out here, but I can't. I'm late for an appointment. I've got to get going."

With that, he was up and walking toward the door before I could stop him, leaving his coffee behind.

I waited just long enough so that I could get lost in the crowd on the sidewalk, and then I followed.

He'd told me he was stopping by a friend's apartment. Now, suddenly, it was an appointment he was late for? I trailed him back to Broadway, keeping my umbrella low enough so that he wouldn't see my face if he turned around . . . which he didn't. He just shouldered his way purposefully through the Saturday crowd until he reached Fiftieth Street, where he turned west.

I guess it never occurred to him that the illustrious mayor of New York would be sidling along behind him, keeping him under surveillance like a private eye in a dime-store novel.

He stopped in front of a construction site, where the sidewalk was covered with a plywood awning. I ducked behind a newsstand two-thirds of a block away and kept my eye on Patrelli. I saw that someone was waiting there for him; a skinny man wearing a backward baseball cap and carrying a satchel. There was a brief conversation between them; then Patrelli reached into his pocket and handed something to the stranger. As he put his hand back into his pocket, I glimpsed something clutched in his fingers.

Now he was walking away and so was the person he'd met there, both heading in opposite directions. I followed Patrelli, who went straight back to the theater.

Obviously, he was up to something. But whether it had anything to do with Matthews's death was impossible to tell at this point.

I checked my watch and saw that I'd better find a cab if I intended to make my next engagement: lunch with Nolan MacDougall.

"To what do I owe the pleasure of this rendezvous?" MacDougall asked. We were seated across from each other in a corner of Gallagher's Steak House, and a waiter had just taken our orders.

I'd chosen this restaurant for two reasons: one, it was close to the theater and I knew MacDougall would be in a hurry to get over there for the matinee; and two, I had an intense craving for a thick piece of red meat. Last night's benefit dinner had consisted of disappointingly light, healthy fare: grilled swordfish and summer vegetables, with fresh berries for dessert. Tasty, but hardly filling.

"I thought we could discuss the Matthews case," I told MacDougall, who was waiting for a reply as he spread his napkin on his lap.

"So I figured." Matthews made a face. "It's all I've been able to think about for days. You have no idea what this is doing to me. My life is turning upside down. First I lost my leading man; now my leading lady. And though both understudies are . . ." He cleared his throat meaningfully, "competent, I'm afraid I'm going to have to recast the roles as soon as possible."

"Beau Walton will be taking over the Quincy Tate role, then?"

He blinked. "Where did you hear that?"

"I have my sources," I said smugly, though it was actually just a hunch. "When are you going to let Patrelli know?"

"No one knows yet, Mr. Mayor," he said with a frown, "and I'd appreciate if you'd keep it to yourself. I don't want the world finding out before Jonathan does."

"What do you think of Jonathan?"

"He's very talented and has an incredible level of energy. He sizzles onstage, and I think he has a wonderful voice . . ." MacDougall paused, and his unspoken *but* hung in the air between us. I voiced it myself, questioningly, when he didn't.

"*But* he's not star material," MacDougall replied. "He simply doesn't have what it takes to carry the show. He's a bit too . . . scattered."

"How so?"

He sighed. "This is just between you and me, but I strongly suspect that Jonathan is using drugs. His behavior is erratic and there are times when he shows up and he isn't . . . all there."

I thought back to Jonathan's clandestine street-corner meeting I'd just witnessed. A drug habit made sense, and it would explain why I sensed that he was hiding something. I didn't want to completely rule him out as a suspect, but he certainly wasn't number one.

"What about Toni Gatto, the understudy who took over Kellie Farrell's role?" I asked Nolan, filing away what he'd said about Patrelli.

"She's fine, when she doesn't have laryngitis. She has a sweet voice and she's graceful. But no one," MacDougall said with a sad shake of his head, "has the stage presence of Kellie. I can hardly believe she was swept out from beneath my nose, that she'll never bring Amber Blue to life on my stage again. I so wanted her to continue in this production. In fact, I had her in mind for a lead in my next show, which will be going into development soon. One doesn't encounter a performer like Kellie Farrell every day; an actress who can sing and dance as well as she acts, who is lithe and beautiful yet not untouchable; who has both strength and vulnerability. We're going to miss her."

"I'm sure you will." I was a little taken aback by his effusive praise of Kellie, and found myself wondering if he were simply trying to throw me off so that I'd conclude there was no way he'd ever frame her for murder.

Then again, Nolan MacDougall is one of the most theatrical men I've ever known. He pretty much goes overboard on everything he says and does.

"Did you see yesterday's newspapers?" he asked me.

"I see the papers every day. I'm the mayor," I reminded him. "What about them?"

He sighed. "Kellie's arrest in the midst of a show was front-page news. And my name was bandied about like a tennis ball at Wimbledon. They're all feeling sorry for me, knowing how dreadfully difficult it is to have your star whisked away the way Kellie was. You can imagine what I'm going through."

"I can imagine."

He shook his head sadly. "This whole business is giving me terrible heartburn, and I haven't slept in weeks. I guess I'll be all right in time, though. I just need to take it easy, calm down, get back down to business."

I marveled at his ability to perceive what had happened as a personal tragedy, never once voicing his sadness for a young man who'd been cut down in the prime of his life, or for a young woman who may have been falsely accused of murder. Was that an indication that he had the ruthless, cold heart of a murderer . . . or simply the tactless soul of a true narcissist?

Our waiter appeared with drinks and rolls. I'd ordered a Diet Coke, and Nolan was having Perrier with a twist.

"What do you think is going to happen to the box office, now that Kellie's gone?" I asked Nolan in an effort to feel him out a bit more.

"Oh, it's going to explode, without a doubt," he said enthusiastically, looking up from the roll he was layering with butter. "We were already sold out for weeks in advance, ever since Conor was killed. Thanks to this latest scandal, you won't be able to get a ticket from now until Doomsday."

Then, perhaps catching the expression on my face, he quickly added, "Of course, it's a shame that it took such a calamity to bring my show back to life. I would trade a decade's worth of box office receipts if it would bring Conor Matthews back."

Oh, sure. And I'd trade a year's salary to spend a month alone on a desert island with Nolan MacDougall.

The guy was an insufferable boor, and he didn't have a sympathetic, caring bone in his body. His only remorse for Matthews's death was probably that it hadn't happened sooner, at the height of tourist season.

I wouldn't put it past him to murder someone for his own benefit. But *had* he? I couldn't be sure.

"How is Beau Walton taking all of this?" I asked, shifting gears. "He must be thrilled to be coming back to Broadway."

"He's quite excited about it, yes. Of course, the man would do anything for me. He owes me his career, and he knows it. I'm the one who spotted him at an obscure little theater on Long Beach Island that long-ago summer night. I made him a star when I cast him as Quincy Tate. It's a wonderful feeling to be able to make someone's dream come true."

"I'll bet."

By the time my steak arrived, I had lost my appetite, thanks to Nolan's sickening monologue about his many personal and professional achievements. I still didn't know whether he was behind Matthews's murder, but my instinct—if I dared trust it—was to doubt it. He seemed too wrapped up in himself to devote the necessary time to something as complicated as plotting and executing the perfect murder.

Before I left the restaurant, I interrupted his tale of a recent shopping trip to Paris, asking him for Beau Walton's home telephone number. He didn't even bother to ask me why I needed it, so eager was he to get back to his favorite topic: himself.

THIRTEEN

I spent Sunday at the San Genarro festival down in Little Italy, and it was wonderful, as usual. The sun was shining and the temperature hovered in the high seventies, with a cool breeze; perfect weather for strolling up and down Mulberry Street. I indulged in pizza and fried bread dough and sausage heroes with peppers and onions, and went through a whole roll of antacid tablets that night as I caught up on paperwork in my office at Gracie Mansion.

Later, as I lay in bed unable to sleep—thanks to heartburn and the Matthews case—I went over and over the details in my mind.

I hadn't yet spoken again to Kellie Farrell or her lawyer, but I knew one of them would contact me as soon as some news was available from the handwriting experts. According to the papers, bail had been denied for Kellie, which wasn't surprising.

Along with their sensational coverage—which included exclusive interviews with Kellie's across-the-hall neighbors and an Indiana couple for whose children she babysat as a teenager—the tabloids had printed excerpts from the letters and journal Matthews had written . . . or should I say, *supposedly* written.

I have to admit that I was just about convinced that Kellie Farrell really was telling the truth; that she'd been framed. I fully expected the experts to come back with the report that the letters had been forged.

Of course, it's not easy to do something like that. You'd have to carefully study someone's handwriting in order to imitate it so extensively; you'd have to practice and you'd have to spend hours creating the forgeries.

Still, I knew, having seen samples that were printed in the papers, that Matthews's writing wasn't particularly distinct or elaborate. He printed; his letters slanting toward the right. His writing was small and his capitals were the same size as the lower-case letters. I know countless men whose handwriting is similar.

If the experts found evidence of forgery, there would still be the matter of the bullets the detectives found in Kellie's dressing room. But those could have easily been planted there; they alone wouldn't be enough to convict her. What they needed was a witness; so far, no one had come forward.

Meanwhile, what I needed was evidence that someone really had framed her, if that was the case. I had a number of suspects, but nothing concrete that I could use against them.

The killer's fingerprints had to be the unexplained ones that were found on the gun, and since they weren't Kellie's, didn't that mean she wasn't the killer?

No, it only meant that someone besides her, and Dan, and Wesley, had handled the prop. Who was it? Unfortunately, it wasn't legal, not to mention practical, for me to get fingerprint samples from all of my suspects and match them against those found on the gun.

My thoughts kept meandering back to Wesley Fisk. He had kept a low profile since Kellie's arrest, though he had continued to perform in the show. I had tried to reach him several times over the weekend, but hadn't been successful. I wanted to speak to him in person, to see how he was handling the fact that the woman he supposedly loved had been put into prison for a crime she denied committing.

The fact that Kellie hadn't contacted him told me that she no longer trusted him completely. She had to believe that Fisk might have been the one who framed her. . . .

But why would he?

That was what troubled me. His only motive for killing Matthews would be to get rid of his rival for Kellie's affections. He wouldn't gain anything from killing Matthews and putting Kellie away for the crime . . . would he?

The whole thing was so complicated it made me exhausted, and yet I couldn't seem to tear my thoughts away.

Again, as the long night wore on and became the wee hours of Monday morning, I was haunted by the feeling that I wasn't seeing the big picture—that there were clues I was overlooking.

When I finally did fall asleep, I dreamed that I was a little boy again, fishing with my father at a lake near the Catskills bungalow colony where we spent summer vacations. In the dream, I kept getting bites on my line, but every time I tried to reel in the enormous trout, it got away, jumping across the water as my father shouted, "There it is, Eddie! Get him! Get him!"

Finally, I threw my fishing pole aside and dove into the ice-cold water, swimming furiously after the fish.

Of course, I didn't catch it.

Not in the dream.

But when the alarm went off that Monday morning, I had every intention of capturing whatever it was that kept eluding me, because I was certain that it was the key that would unlock the case.

I placed a call to Artie Masters first thing when I reached my office that morning, but he didn't call me back until midafternoon. He said he'd just gotten in from L.A., where he'd been negotiating a movie deal for one of his clients.

"What can I do for you, Ed?" he asked.

I grimaced at the sound of my first name on his lips. We barely knew each other, yet he was the type who'd want to be old friends right away. Sybil had told me he was a notorious name-dropper, famous for buddying up to virtual strangers and then telling the world, the next day, about his fabulous "friend."

I said tersely, "Actually, I wanted to discuss something with you—"

"Great! Let's do lunch. I'm free on—"

I interrupted promptly, bursting his bubble. "I can just ask you over the phone, to tell you the truth, Artie. I had a question about Conor Matthews's career."

"Conor?" He sounded subdued. "What about him?"

"I just wondered whether he was thinking of leaving the cast of *The Last Laugh* before he died."

He hedged a bit. "Well, we both knew the show wasn't going to last forever. It was no secret that Conor's reviews weren't exactly *sterling*. I had other things in mind for him, yes."

"Had you sent him any scripts to read? You know, for auditions?"

"No, I hadn't. Why do you ask?"

"I was just curious. I heard through the grapevine that Conor might be auditioning for a revival of *Crimes of the Heart*," I said, and waited for his reaction.

"Crimes of the Heart?" he echoed dubiously. "I doubt that's the sort of thing Conor would turn to at this stage in his career. If anything, he dearly wanted to return to Shakespearean theater. I thought everyone knew that."

"Mmm," I said noncommittally. "So you don't think Conor was going to try another contemporary drama?"

"I *know* he wasn't," Artie said. "Who on earth told you that he was?"

"As I said, I just heard it through the grapevine. Oh, there's my other line," I lied, then thanked him and hung up as he was protesting.

Next on my list of phone calls was Beau Walton. I reached him just as he returned from the gym on Monday afternoon, and he sounded surprised to hear from me. Obviously, Nolan MacDougall had neglected to tell him I'd asked for his number.

"What can I do for you, Mr. Mayor?" he asked politely, but there was an edge to his voice.

"I was wondering if we could get together tonight for a quick drink," I said. "I thought you might be able to help me with something."

"Oh? Like what? Do you want me to do a commercial for the Manhattan Tourism board, or something?"

I almost laughed, but managed to turn it into a cough. "Er, no," I said seriously, "I just wanted to ask you a few questions."

"What about?"

Might as well be straightforward, I thought.

"About Conor Matthews," I told him.

"What about him?"

"Can we meet in person? I really don't like to get into this sort of thing on the phone."

He sighed. "I'm really busy . . ."

"It won't take long."

"All right," he said. "Where do you want to meet?"

"Where do you live?"

"East Eighty-third Street between First and York."

"Convenient," I said. "That's my neighborhood."

I named a small Italian restaurant I liked to go to, and he knew where it was. We agreed to meet at the bar there at seven.

That would give me almost an hour to question him before I had to be across town for a movie opening that I really didn't want to miss. The film, *Brooklyn Dreaming,* had been shot entirely on location in Park Slope, and I had done a cameo, playing myself of course, as a favor to the director. Stan Kruger and I had gone to Hebrew School together as children in Newark, and we'd lost touch for years, until he made it big in Hollywood and I made it big in politics. Now, whenever he filmed a movie in New York, he pestered me to appear, but my schedule hadn't allowed me to do that until recently.

I spent the rest of the afternoon and early evening in conference with my fiscal advisors and was ten minutes late meeting Walton.

I found him sitting on a stool toward the back of the bar. He wore an actor's uniform of a black turtleneck with a tweed blazer and snug-fitting black jeans, his longish hair stylishly combed back with a liberal dollop of gel. He was surrounded by three admiring females, all of them in black spandex miniskirts with mile-long legs.

Beau was obviously basking in their attention and didn't look thrilled to see me. Whether it was because I was interrupting his little fan club or because he was reluctant to discuss the Matthews case, I couldn't tell. Probably a little of both.

When we were alone and the bartender, whose name is also Ed—which in his book makes us kin—had brought me a glass of my favorite red wine, I glanced at my watch and said, "I'm going to make this quick, Mr. Walton."

"I figured. You're probably headed for that Kruger opening, huh?"

"How did you know?"

"I heard you had a cameo in it. Stan Kruger's a friend of yours, huh?"

"Yes, he is . . . do you know him?"

"I auditioned for that film, but it wasn't right for me. It was just too slapstick," Walton added.

I figured that meant he hadn't been chosen for the role. When talking to an actor with an ego like Walton's, you have to read between the lines.

I cleared my throat and changed the subject. "I hear you're going back to *The Last Laugh.*"

He raised an eyebrow at me. "Good news travels fast in this town."

"When you're the mayor, you tend to hear things ahead of the masses," I told him. "Congratulations."

"Thank you. It was something I really just couldn't refuse. I mean, I made the role of Quincy Tate famous, and I guess the world won't be happy until I return to the stage. Besides, I couldn't turn Nolan down. He's suffered quite a few blows lately. I have to help him out."

"What about your film career?"

"Oh . . . er, that's going to be put on hold for the time being. I hate to disappoint the movie industry, but there's only so much of me to go around."

If I hadn't been sitting next to him, witnessing verbal evidence of his shameless vanity, I wouldn't have believed anyone really spoke this way. He and Nolan MacDougall had obviously been cut from the same cloth.

"Who do you think killed Conor Matthews?" I asked him, watching carefully for his reaction.

I had caught him off guard; that was evident in the way his eyes widened. But he quickly resumed his composure and said, sounding mildly surprised, "Wasn't Kellie Farrell just arrested for his murder?"

"She was, but she hadn't been convicted yet, has she?"

"No, I guess she hasn't." He took a gulp of his drink, something amber-colored. Stiff, too, judging by the way he winced as he swallowed it.

"Do you think she's guilty?" I asked him.

"To tell you the truth, I don't know her very well," he said.

"What about Wesley Fisk?"

An expression of distaste slid across his handsome features. "What about him?"

"Do you know him well?"

"Yes, of course I do. He was with the show long before I left."

"What do you think of him?"

"I think that if anyone was capable of killing Matthews, Fisk was," he said. "The man is a pompous ass, with an ego the size of Madison Square Garden."

I raised an eyebrow and an old saying about pots and kettles darted through my mind.

"So you're saying that you suspect Wesley Fisk of the murder?" was all I said.

"I did, until they arrested someone else," he said.

"Why did you think he might be guilty?"

"Everyone in town knew he was sleeping with Matthews's fiancée. And he's the cutthroat type in his professional life. It made sense that he'd kill the competition in his personal life, too. I tried to tell Nolan that, but he didn't want to hear it. He can't afford to lose another leading performer in that show at this point. It's going to be up to me to save it as it is."

"I thought it was sold out for months in advance."

"Well, that's just because of the sensationalism surrounding the show ever since the murder. It can only carry the box office for so long," he said. "What *The Last Laugh* needs is to be revitalized by new talent."

"Namely, you."

"Namely, me," he agreed, and drained his glass. He raised an index finger and beckoned to the bartender. Ed was busy with other customers and didn't see him.

"Excuse me, bartender!" Walton called. The bartender ignored him.

"What's his problem?" Walton wondered, clearly irritated that the bartender hadn't dropped everything to rush over and cater to his whim. "Is he deaf?"

"No, he isn't. I'm sure he'll be with you when he has a chance." Walton grumbled and fiddled with his empty glass.

"Do you know what people are saying about you?" I couldn't resist asking.

"Hold that thought," he said to me, as Ed appeared in front of us. "I'll have another brandy," Walton commanded. "Straight up. And make it fast."

"Anything for you, Mr. Mayor?" Ed asked me, clearly wondering what I was doing keeping company with such a jerk.

"No, thanks, I'm fine." I sipped my wine. "How are Nancy and the kids?"

"Same old, same old. Joey just got his driver's license. I told him that's going to be the death of me. How are things at City Hall?"

"Same old, same old there, too," I said with a grin.

Walton, who was growing impatient with both the bartender and me, nudged my arm and asked, "What are they saying?"

"Excuse me?" I said, as if I hadn't the foggiest notion what he was talking about.

"What are people saying about me?" He was wearing a slight smile, looking like he expected a heap of praise.

Naturally, I relished informing him that some people thought he might have had something to do with the murder.

He looked horrified, and shocked. In fact, if he hadn't been a professional actor, I would have taken his reaction to mean that he was innocent of any connection to the murder. But since he made his living manufacturing false emotions, I couldn't quite give him the benefit of the doubt.

"That's the most ridiculous thing I've ever heard," he said. "Why would I kill Conor Matthews? I barely knew him."

"Because your film career wasn't taking off and you were desperate to come back to the show, but he was in your way?" I said, and added hastily, "You understand, that's not me talking. I'm just repeating what I've heard."

"Well, it's crazy," Walton said. "I had no reason to kill off

Matthews if I wanted to come back. All I'd have to do is say the word."

"But I heard Matthews had a contract."

He shrugged. "In this business, there's a way around everything. Believe me, Mr. Mayor, I'm hardly desperate. A man like Beau Walton doesn't have to go around killing people in order to get work. I'm one of the most successful actors ever on Broadway."

I could have argued that point, but why bother? I was already running late.

I pushed my still-full wineglass across the bar, hopped off my stool, and said, "I'm sorry to cut this short, but I have to run. I'm late for my movie opening. Shall I tell Stan you sent your regards?"

"Uh, that's not necessary," he said as Ed set his drink in front of him.

"Are you sure? He's casting a new film now. I could put in a good word for you if—oh, that's right. You're going to be busy on Broadway now."

"I certainly am." Walton reached for his glass and drained half of it in a single gulp. "I hope you'll set straight anyone who has the nerve to speculate that I might have had something to do with the murder, Mr. Mayor."

"Of course I will, Mr. Walton. Oh, and break a leg."

And believe me, I meant that with all my heart.

Sybil and Claude were at the opening, and she wasted no time in rushing over to me at the reception held directly after the screening.

"Ed! You were wonderful," she exclaimed.

I rolled my eyes. "All I did was say one line, Sybil."

"Yes, but the way you said it," she teased me. "Will you give me a private encore?"

"Why not?" I spread my arms and said, with feeling, " 'How'm I doing?' "

She grinned and gave me a thumbs-up. "Oscar material, Ed."

"Thanks."

"Listen," she said, lowering her voice, "how's the case coming?"

"I'm still working on it. No new leads."

"But you think Kellie Farrell's innocent?"

"I didn't say that."

"If you didn't think it, you wouldn't still be working on the case," she reasoned, plucking a bacon-wrapped scallop off a passing waiter's tray. "I'm anxious to hear what those handwriting experts say about the letters."

"You're not the only one." They were supposed to have finished their analysis today, but so far I'd heard nothing. I had spoken with Amanda just before leaving City Hall earlier, and she'd promised to let me know as soon as she heard something. She'd also said Kellie was despondent.

Still munching on her scallop, Sybil snatched another hors d'oeuvre and caught me raising my eyebrow.

"I'm starved," she explained. "I had a rock-scaling session just before I got ready to come to the movie, and there wasn't time for dinner."

"Where does one scale rocks in Manhattan?" I asked.

"It was actually at the gym," she said. "They have one of those walls with pegs for you to grab onto, you know, as practice. I'm in training for the trip Claude and I are taking to the Alps next month."

"Just thinking about it makes me exhausted," I told her.

"You should try it, Ed."

"Rock climbing? Me?" I shook my head. "I have enough challenges just running this city every day, Sybil."

"And trying to solve murder cases."

"That, too," I agreed.

"Are you getting close?" she wanted to know.

"I think so. There's just some detail I'm overlooking," I told her. "I can't get past the feeling that if I could just remember it, I'd have the key to the puzzle."

"Maybe you're on the wrong track. Maybe the police are right, and Kellie really did kill him, and that's all there is to it."

"Maybe," I agreed.

But I honestly didn't think so.

That's why it was a shock for me to return home late that evening and find a message from Amanda Filbert on my voice mail.

"Ed," she said, her voice sounding hollow, "I just heard from my handwriting expert. They've finished analyzing both the letters and the journal entries. They've concluded that they aren't forgeries—they really were written by Matthews."

FOURTEEN

On Tuesday, I had to be in Albany for that meeting with the governor by nine a.m. I was supposed to fly, but the airports were fogged in, so I found myself being driven up the Taconic Parkway during rush hour.

The car trip gave me plenty of time to prepare for the meeting . . . and to think about the Matthews case. I kept telling myself that it was over—that Kellie Farrell was, quite obviously, guilty.

And yet, I couldn't seem to accept that the case was closed. I kept remembering how certain I'd been of her innocence. I kept hearing her voice saying, "I'm telling you the truth, Mr. Mayor." I kept seeing her face, the way she'd looked me directly in the eye.

She hadn't done any of the telltale things people do when they're lying. There had been no hesitancy in her voice, no fidgeting or blushing or repetition of my questions. She had been the picture of integrity.

And obviously, she had pulled one over on me.

During the meeting, I found myself having difficulty concentrating on the budget discussion. My mind kept wandering back to Kellie, to how she'd probably spend the rest of her life in prison . . . if she was lucky. New York had recently reinstated the death penalty, and I wondered if the prosecution would be seeking it in the Matthews case.

Finally, it was evening and the meeting was over. I settled into the back seat of the limo and asked Mohammed to tune the radio to an easy-listening station I always enjoy. I hadn't slept well in several nights, and I found myself yawning as the music washed over me.

"That was Barbra Streisand with 'People Who Need People,' " the announcer's velvety voice said. "Now, let's change the pace with a tune from the Broadway show, *The Last Laugh*. Here's Beau Walton singing, 'Hug Me, Hugo.' "

I sat upright. This damned case was haunting me. Would I ever have a moment's peace again?

As the familiar lyrics filled the car, I found myself singing along mentally. And I heard Conor Matthews's voice in my mind, remembering the way he'd flubbed the lyrics during that final performance.

He'd been drinking that night. Now I knew why. He must have been distraught over the knowledge that, not only was the woman he loved in love with someone else, but she was trying to kill him. That was enough to drive anyone to drink.

As Beau Walton's recorded voice sang the line "Hug Me, Hugo," over and over in the song's chorus, I was hearing Conor Matthews slurring it as he had the night he'd died.

And then it struck me . . .

Had he really been just slurring?

Or had he been saying something else—something other than "Hug Me, Hugo?"

There was only one way to find out.

Traffic on the FDR was horrendous, thanks to a terrible accident involving a gypsy cab and a garbage truck. By the time we reached Gracie Mansion, it was nearly midnight.

I knew I had an early breakfast meeting in the morning. What I should have done, I thought as I tossed my briefcase on the floor just inside my bedroom door, was gone straight to bed. A person can only run on coffee and adrenaline for so many days before he crashes.

But I knew I wouldn't be able to sleep once again. Not until I found out whether my memory was misleading me.

So I found the videotape of Conor Matthews's last performance, and I fast-forwarded it until I reached the end of Act One. I pressed Play just as Matthews began singing "Hug Me, Hugo."

Except, he wasn't singing "Hugo" at all.

I had to hit Rewind and Play several times to be sure, but I ultimately concluded that there was no doubt about it.

What Matthews was saying was "Hug me, *Iago.*"

Iago, as anyone who's read Shakespeare's *Othello* knows, was the title character's so-called friend, whom he calls a man "of honesty and trust." But the audience knows that Iago hates Othello. It is because of Iago that Othello's true love, the beautiful Desdemona, betrays him with infidelity.

What happens next in the play is truly shattering, which is why it's considered by some to be one of Shakespeare's most tragic masterpieces.

And, as I sat pondering the plot . . .

And the fact that Conor Matthews had told Sybil that his most triumphant stage role had been his portrayal of Othello . . .

And the memory of the incongruous pile of scripts in his office . . .

And the books . . .

And Conor Matthews's relationship with his mother . . .

Everything fell into place.

The explanation was so startlingly simple—and the killer's identity so shocking—that I found myself shaking my head, not wanting to believe it.

And yet, another part of me wanted desperately to believe it, because it would mean that I'd been right about Kellie Farrell all along.

If my hunch was correct, she really was innocent.

Now all I had to do was prove it.

And I had a very good idea of how I might be able to do that. . . .

Wednesday, as soon as my breakfast meeting was over, I called Sebastian Nicolay's office.

"I'm sorry, Mr. Mayor," his secretary said politely. "Mr. Nicolay and his wife are in Europe until the end of the month."

"Do you have a number where they can be reached?"

"No, I don't. He does call in to check his messages, though. Would you like me to have him contact you?"

"Please," I said, though I knew I couldn't wait that long.

I was scheduled to leave Thursday evening for Washington, then go on to Dallas for that political conference. I had just over twenty-four hours to wrap up the Matthews case and free Kellie Farrell.

I would have loved to have visited her in prison, or even to have called her lawyer to tell her that I thought I'd cracked the case. But I didn't for two reasons.

The first is that there just wasn't time. I had a packed schedule on Wednesday, right up until the museum benefit banquet I was scheduled to attend this evening.

The second reason is that I didn't want to risk getting Kellie's hopes up if I couldn't find the proof I needed.

I suppose there was always the chance that I was wrong . . . that my theory was utterly ridiculous.

But I didn't allow myself to consider that.

My conclusion made sense, and besides, my gut instinct was telling me that I was right.

The same gut instincts that had told me that Kellie Farrell was innocent. . . .

The gut instinct that had guided me and landed me where I am today: mayor of the greatest city in the world.

I had to take a gamble and trust myself. If I was right, I'd save an innocent woman from punishment for a crime she didn't commit.

And if I was wrong . . .

Well, if I was wrong, then I didn't deserve to be mayor of the greatest city in the world after all.

It was pouring rain when I managed to duck out of the banquet, and nearly eight-thirty. I had my bodyguards drive me back to Gracie Mansion, and made a show of going up to my room as if I were going to bed.

But upstairs, I paged Mohammed Johnson, who hadn't been on duty tonight. Of all my guards, he's the most closed-mouthed . . .

and the most athletic. I needed both of those qualifications for what I had planned.

When he answered my page, I asked him if he felt like going on a little adventure.

"If it's a safe adventure, I'm with you, Mr. Mayor," he said, and I assured him that I had no intention of risking my neck. I asked him to meet me at the back of the mansion as soon as he could get there, and I told him to wear something comfortable—and dark.

Then I changed my own clothes and went down the back staircase. In one hand, I held a flashlight; in the other, the keys to my own car, which I rarely drive these days.

The last thing I wanted was to be accompanied by an entourage, where I was going. I didn't need any witnesses, and besides, I didn't feel like explaining what I was up to. But I wasn't fool enough to venture far without at least one bodyguard. I'd tried that back when I was first mayor, with disastrous results that I won't go into here. Just allow me to say that I was lucky to be alive to see another term in office.

Mohammed—who asked no questions, just as I'd expected—took the wheel and I sat in the front seat beside him. The guard seemed surprised as we drove past the gatehouse, but let us go with just a wave and a smile.

I had Mohammed cut through Central Park, then take the West Side Highway up to the George Washington Bridge.

Traffic was light at this time of night, in this weather, and before long, we were crossing the Hudson and entering New Jersey.

I have always prided myself in having an excellent memory when it comes to geography. I know New York and its suburbs like the back of my hand, and I can find my way around most major American cities, even those I've only visited once or twice. When I was a kid in the car with my parents, taking a Sunday drive, my father would inevitably get us lost, and my mother would inevitably say, "Why don't you ask Eddie which way to go? He always knows where we are."

And I always did.

Tonight, despite the rain and the many years that had passed since I'd been there, I managed to find my way back to the Nicolays' sprawling estate near South Orange. It looked just as I remembered it: a large white house set back from the road and bordered by a low fieldstone wall. The house was lit and so were the twin lampposts flanking the drive, and at first I thought someone might be home.

I had Mohammed park the car and wait while I splashed through the rain to the front door. They've never had live-in help, and I knew the place had to be empty. The lights were probably set on timers, to thwart thieves.

I felt a little guilty as I returned to the car and told Mohammed to pull around to the back of the house. After all, I was an intruder, and I knew what I was doing was, technically, trespassing.

But I had no choice, I reminded myself. I had to solve this case, and sooner was better than later.

The guest house was tucked at the back of the property, behind a two-story carriage house. It, like the main residence, was a white clapboard structure with a porch and two chimneys, but everything was on a smaller scale.

I thought of Conor Matthews walking in the door of that house and finding his mother dead inside, and I shuddered.

You don't forget pain like that. Even if you don't break down outwardly, you carry the memory with you. You're haunted by it, and it eats away at you for years until one day, you realize you can't live with it anymore.

"So what's up, Mr. Mayor? What are we doing?" Mohammed's quietly-spoken question snapped me out of my reverie.

"I'll explain when I know exactly," I told him. "For now, wait right here." I hated to make him venture out into the driving rain.

"No, I'll come along," he said in a no-nonsense voice, and I shrugged, knowing it was his job.

I opened the car door and stepped onto the walk leading up to the guest house.

But that wasn't where I was headed.

Motioning to Mohammed, I moved past it. The grass was soggy and squished beneath the soles of my loafers as I picked my way across the yard toward the deep stand of trees that edged the property. There were so many of them, and though the leaves were starting to turn, the branches were still lush, the treetops hidden.

It might be impossible to find what I was looking for, I realized as I played the light overhead, rain soaking my upward-tilted face.

Or maybe it no longer existed. Maybe it was long-gone, like Mindy and Conor Matthews themselves.

Besides, I reminded myself, even if I found it, I might not find the clue I was counting on. I could be completely off base . . .

There!

The ray of my flashlight had just caught something in a tree high above my head, something that wasn't a branch or a leaf.

I steadied the beam and saw that it was still there, all right, even after all these years.

Conor Matthews's tree house.

There was the little porch Sebastian Nicolay had told me about, and there was the little mailbox . . .

And yes, there, I hoped, was the clue I was looking for. Relief coursed through me as I zeroed in on it . . .

The small red flag that someone had lifted so that it pointed straight up.

It didn't mean anything for certain, I reminded myself as I strode toward the trunk of the tree. But there was a good chance . . .

I stopped dead at the base of the tree.

Every part of the tree house was intact, except the most important.

The makeshift ladder Sebastian had told me he'd constructed by nailing small wedges of wood to the trunk. I could see ridges and holes in the bark where they must have been, but it appeared that someone had ripped them out—and recently, judging by the marks.

Filled with frustration, I stared up at the mailbox that hovered so tantalizingly close . . . and yet, it might as well be at the top of Mount Everest. There was no way I could reach it.

"What's going on, Mr. Mayor?" Mohammed, who was two steps behind me, called over the sound of the rain.

"I know this seems crazy," I said, "but I need to get up that tree."

"Looks like that's not going to be possible without a ladder," he said. "I'd try to get up there without one, by grabbing onto one of those branches, but my doctor would have my head. He made me give up doing pull-ups ever since I wrecked my elbow back in college football ten years back. Had to have surgery in ninety-two after I ignored his advice and went hang gliding. If we had a ladder, though . . ."

"I know."

I glanced helplessly toward the carriage house, wondering if Sebastian had a ladder in there. Even if he did, I thought as I strode toward it, the doors were probably locked.

Of course, they were.

There was only one thing left to do.

I had to call the one person I knew who was capable of scaling a rain-slick tree trunk without asking too many questions first.

"If I do this," Sybil said, putting on a pair of gloves and staring up the giant old oak, "I get to write whatever I want for tomorrow's column."

"As long as it's the truth," I promised her, as Mohammed stood silently by, keeping watch. "And if that mailbox is concealing what I think it is, you're about to get one hell of an exclusive."

"What if it's empty?"

"Then you're about to get one hell of a workout," I told her, and protested, "You said you were in training for the Alps," when she gave me a nasty look.

"You're lucky I was home when you called," she told me. "And that Claude is out of town, because he wouldn't have been crazy about my driving to Jersey and climbing a tree just because you asked me to."

"I am lucky," I told her. "Thank you."

"You're welcome," she said. "But I'm telling you, Ed, this had better be good."

"I couldn't agree with you more."

"Here goes nothing."

I watched with fascination and admiration as Sybil shimmied up the tree trunk with relatively little effort. At the top, she stepped gingerly onto the platform of the tree house and took off her right glove.

"Check the mailbox," I called up to her.

"What do you think I'm going to do? Play Tarzan?" she shot back.

I watched as she reached with what seemed like agonizing slowness for the lid of the rounded box. She tugged on it and hollered down to me, "It's all rusty."

"What do you expect? Does it open?"

"It opens," she replied, even as she swung the lid downward and reached inside.

I held my breath as I waited, and images flashed through my mind.

I saw red staining Conor Matthews's shirt as bullets struck him in the chest.

I saw Kellie Farrell holding his bleeding body as she sat on the stage floor.

I saw her breaking into a relieved smile when I told her that I believed she was telling the truth.

I saw Richard Matthews's eyes narrowed with disgust as he told me how his ex-wife had taken her own life.

I saw Tetty Nicolay shaking her head sadly as she told me how close Conor and his mother had been, how they used to leave notes for each other in the tree house mailbox . . .

"I've got something!" Sybil shouted suddenly. "It looks like a letter."

FIFTEEN

"Mr. Mayor!"

I was just about to hand my ticket to the gate attendant when I heard someone calling my name. There was nothing unusual about that—ever since I'd arrived at La Guardia fifteen minutes earlier to catch the shuttle to Washington, I'd been waylaid by one person after another, some of them acquaintances, some reporters, but most total strangers.

They all wanted to know the same thing:

How had I known where to find Conor Matthews's suicide note?

And I had given everyone who asked the same answer:

Intuition.

It had been a long day and now, thanks to Sybil's exclusive interview with me, which had appeared in this morning's *Register,* I could hardly wait to escape New York, much as I loved it, for a while.

But once again, someone called, "Mr. Mayor! Please, wait!"

I turned with a sigh and prepared to go through the same routine once more before boarding the plane.

"Thank goodness I caught you," said the woman who had called my name, stopping as she reached me.

"Kellie!" I was truly shocked to see her. "What are you doing here?"

"I had to thank you in person," she said, pausing to catch her breath, "Your secretary told Amanda where you were, but I didn't think I could get here on time."

"You almost didn't. My flight leaves in a few minutes."

"I know. I ran across the airport. I just wanted to say that I owe you . . . God, I owe you everything! If you hadn't figured out that Conor had killed himself, I'd still be sitting in that horrible jail cell now."

"When did you get out?"

"As soon as the police confirmed that the handwriting in the suicide note was authentic, and that the fingerprints on the gun were Conor's."

"Did you read the note?" I asked her. I had, of course. It had been addressed to his mother, a rambling letter about how painful his life had become and how he would be joining her soon.

Something told me that he'd never intended human eyes to read it, judging by the way he'd ripped the ladder-steps out of the tree trunk so that no one could get up to the tree house. I think that he'd lost touch with reality and retreated, in some part of his demented mind, back to the days when he was a little boy who desperately loved and needed his mommy. He'd written the note to her, and left it in their private place, knowing that was where she—and she alone—would find it.

Kellie shook her head, her blue eyes clouding over. "I didn't want to read it, Mr. Mayor. I know how much Conor hated me for what I did to him. I don't need to read about it. I can't believe he tried to frame me for his murder. He knew that would destroy my life . . ."

She trailed off, shaking her head. I couldn't tell whether she was sad, or angry, or both.

"Just as Othello destroyed his Desdemona," I said, "before taking *his* own life."

"I can't believe that was what he was doing—lifting the plot of *Othello* to fit his twisted suicide scenario." Her mouth was set grimly. "Conor always was dramatic. But how did you ever piece things together?"

I shrugged. "He left clues."

"The way he called Hugo 'Iago' in the song?"

I nodded. "There were others, too," I told her. "The books and scripts in his dressing room . . . all of them were written by, or about, people who had committed suicide."

"And you think he left them there deliberately?"

"I think he was fascinated with the idea of killing himself. His mother and his grandfather had done it, and he probably always fantasized about it himself. He was in a lot of pain, Kellie," I told her.

"I know that. I told you that for him to start drinking again, he'd have to be at the end of his rope," she said, and then her eyes flashed. "But did he have to take me down with him?"

"You betrayed him," I said. "It was the last straw."

"If he left the clues, you think he figured that eventually, someone would figure out that he'd killed himself?" she asked. "And that I'd be off the hook?"

"I don't know," I acknowledged. "Maybe we never will know. He was so obsessed with suicide that he may have left the books and scripts behind as a careless oversight. He was obviously immersed in them in the days leading up to his death."

"And what about his calling Wesley 'Iago' during the production number?"

"That could have been another careless slip. Remember, he'd been drinking, and he was preoccupied with drawing a parallel between his own life and that of his stage hero, Othello."

"But it could have been deliberate?" She so wanted to believe it, to think that Conor hadn't hated her so much that he'd put her away for life for a crime she didn't commit.

And so I conceded, "Maybe, Kellie, he wanted to be fair to you, and he did leave evidence that he'd taken his own life, hoping it would lead someone to his suicide note."

"*Fair?*" she echoed. "I almost wound up as a candidate for the electric chair for something I didn't do. You call that fair?"

I stared at her, recalling Othello. He, like Conor Matthews, was too blinded by infatuation to realize that the woman he adored was frivolous . . . and fickle. And Kellie Farrell, like the pampered, shallow Desdemona, had been done in by her own weakness of character.

Yet Kellie, unlike Shakespeare's doomed heroine, had been spared.

I could only hope she had learned something from what had happened.

"Are you going back to *The Last Laugh?*" I asked her as the attendant made the final boarding call for my flight.

"No. At least, not just yet. I think I need some time to get myself together . . . and some time away from Wesley. He's so . . . superficial," she said. "He didn't even try to see me while I was under arrest. I guess he thought it would hurt his precious career. I don't know what I ever saw in him. And I was wrong to have cheated on Conor."

I smiled. Maybe she really had changed—or maybe she wasn't as shallow as I'd suspected.

"I have to go now, Kellie," I said, "but you take care of yourself."

"I will," she said, and reached out to shake my hand.

Was it my imagination, or did she grasp my fingers for an unnecessarily long time?

It wasn't my imagination.

No, as I turned to hand my ticket to the waiting attendant and she turned to walk away, I heard her call, "Did you get that, Dayton?"

"Got it," called the tabloid photographer who had stationed himself across the gate area.

There was a flash as he snapped one last shot, then gave me a cheerful wave.

I sighed, envisioning the photograph in tomorrow's paper, accompanied by a caption that would read, *Actress Thanks Mayor For Giving Her Freedom.*

Obviously, I hadn't been wrong about Kellie Farrell. She may not have committed a bloody murder, but she was no saint either.

No, she was, just as I'd suspected, a spotlight-hungry actress who wasn't above taking advantage of a little free publicity.

Ah, well.

I'd solved the case, and that was what mattered.

It was safe for me to go on trusting my instincts, and I was worthy of being Mayor of New York City, after all.

And as long as I'm on the subject . . .

How'm I doing?